# Beyond the Valley of Thorns

THE LAND OF ELYON BOOK 2

# BEYOND THE VALLEY OF THORNS

## PATRICK CARMAN

ORCHARD BOOKS ✦ NEW YORK
An Imprint of Scholastic Inc.

In addition to the people I thanked in *The Dark Hills Divide*, I would like to add the following: Charisse Meloto for her boundless energy and leadership; Jennifer Pasenan, Rachel Coun, and Katy Coyle—their enthusiasm and hard work make me wonder how I got anything done before I met them; Barbara Marcus and Jean Feiwel, for making me feel at home in an unfamiliar place; Remy Wilcox for her critical eye and unwavering support; and to Jeremy Gonzalez, who risked everything on my behalf.

Library of Congress Cataloging-in-Publication Data available

ISBN 0-439-70094-9

12  11  10  9  8  7  6  5  4  3  2  1
05  06  07  08  09

Printed in the U.S.A.  23
First edition, September 2005

*For Sierra*

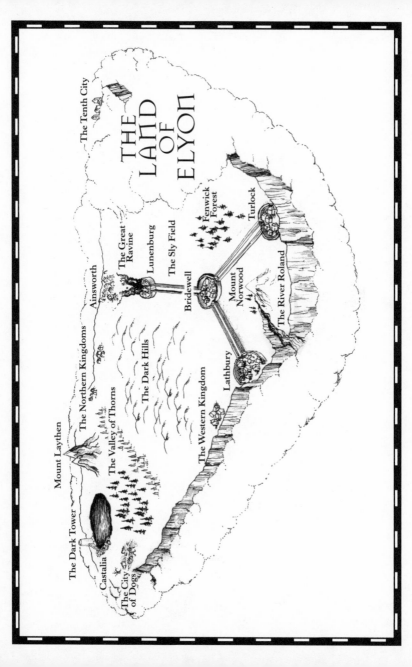

*As evening approaches and the shadows begin their descent into Bridewell, the same frightening thoughts always disturb me. Darkness sends its shadows to draw all men back into itself, for it is in the shadows that darkness plays. And what of the man who stays in the shadows too long, at play with sinister thoughts?*

*Darkness will surely overtake him.*

From the diary of Thomas Warvold

*To be surprised, to wonder, is to begin to understand.*

*The Revolt of the Masses,*
José Ortega y Gasset

# PART I

PART 1

# CHAPTER I

# MY ARRIVAL IN BRIDEWELL

Yesterday I left Lathbury behind. I traveled with Father and he let me drive the cart on the road to Bridewell. The journey could not have been more different from the one I took on the same road only a year ago, before the walls that surrounded it were taken down. The ride is still hot, but yesterday I could see in every direction — the Dark Hills to my left, the valley floor and Mount Norwood to my right, Fenwick Forest a green mass in the distance. As I looked around and smelled the air thick with blooms, I couldn't help but daydream about the adventures that might be had in the faraway corners of The Land of Elyon.

Driving along the dusty road, I kept a lookout for animals I might recognize or hawks flying overhead, but it seemed the animals had been sent into hiding by the noisy grinding of our wagon wheels on the road.

"So, can you tell me the rules once more?" I asked my father. After all the events of the previous summer he was more protective than ever, and I wanted to be sure I knew the rules I'd likely break once we arrived in Bridewell.

"Ah, yes, the rules," he replied, whittling on a stick with his knife. "First and foremost, absolutely no leaving the confines of Bridewell unless accompanied by an adult, and even then I want to know exactly where you're going and why. There's plenty to keep you busy in town without milling around outside unsupervised. And no sneaking around the lodge, listening in on conversations you shouldn't be hearing. Also, you're to join me for dinner each evening. It's time I started grooming you for leadership. A few more years and your visits to Bridewell will be less play and more work."

I could feel my childhood slipping away with each of his statements, most notably the last remark about becoming a leader in our community. It made me long for the days when Warvold had told me stories and I'd been off on adventures in the mountains with Yipes and Murphy. I wished my father wasn't so important, that I was an unknown girl drifting through towns on my way to one place or another, free to travel The Land of Elyon as I pleased.

"Sounds exciting," I replied, faking enthusiasm a bit more than I should have. My father looked at me as if my tone was not what he had hoped for. We settled into a silence, he no doubt thinking of how he might keep an eye on me and still get his work done over the summer, me dreaming of adventures to be had in faraway places.

Half an hour passed with little talk between us, and then the walls of Bridewell came into view a long way down the road. These were the only walls that remained, and their presence seemed to appear out of nowhere, like a giant limbless tree cut to a stump, sitting cold and alone in the wild. I suddenly felt unprotected out in the open, a feeling that had come and gone ever since the walls had been removed everywhere else. Even in the safety of my home along the towering jagged cliffs by the sea, I couldn't seem to shake the feeling that I was somehow unsafe without the walls that I'd been so eager to be rid of only a summer ago.

The horses picked up their pace upon seeing their destination. It wasn't long before we arrived at the huge wooden gate where Pervis Kotcher stood high above in the guard tower. Even at a distance I could see his wiry face and thin mustache. His eyes, always dark and penetrating, watched carefully as my horses came to an abrupt stop in front of the entrance to Bridewell.

"Oh, no. Trouble has arrived along with Mr. Daley," Pervis said to the man at his side. "Best we keep double watch at the towers until she takes her leave."

I smiled up at him, and a flood of memories swirled around in my head. I was back in Bridewell for another summer and my adventurous spirit was newly flamed.

"Nice to see you, too, Pervis," I said. "I'm looking forward to eluding you day after day, all summer long."

We entered Bridewell and the day was filled with the business of settling in at Renny Lodge, unpacking my one bag, and enjoying meals with my father, Nicolas,

Grayson, Silas Hardy, and Pervis. Each of these men had played an important part in my life, especially during the eventful previous summer in Bridewell. My father, ever the leader, was already busy with endless meetings. Nicolas looked trim and handsome as usual, but he was more serious now, and he seemed to have aged more than the year since his own father's death. What can be said of Grayson for those who might have forgotten him? He remained plump, forever sneaking to the kitchen, and I still loved visiting him in the library where he worked at mending books. Silas continued his duties as mail carrier for my father and other important folks, but he had grown into something of a confidant to my father, the two of them often walking together and talking quietly. Pervis had stopped following me around trying to catch me escaping, but I'd never known him to be more alert and cautious of the outside. He spent most of his time at the guard towers, and he seemed to be waiting nervously for something I could only imagine. The only person missing was Ganesh. A year later it was still hard to believe how he had deceived us all.

A day later, with the journey and the greetings behind me, I was able to sit on the sill of the window in my room and think. The walled confines of Bridewell were oddly comforting to me now. To see them from the window in my room or walk around the town square and see the walls all around produced in me a very different feeling than it used to. A year before I could not imagine anything better than escaping those walls; now I couldn't help but enjoy their strong arms encircling me in safety. I could take pleasure in them now as I could not before, especially since I hadn't seen them in a year's time. My hometown of Lathbury was so different, all out in the open, lounging at the edge of the cliffs with room to grow and expand wherever it wanted to. I wondered if I had misjudged these walls as something to fear rather than embrace. When you get what you wish for, it's never quite what you think it will be.

And yet, despite the comfort of the walls, I also wondered what I would find in the Dark Hills, past where I could see. I wondered what lay in the mist beyond Fenwick Forest, if anything at all. The adventurer in me dreamed of escaping once again, only this time I would go much farther, past where our kingdom ended, into lands that only Warvold had traveled and explored.

My daydreaming got me to thinking about the library and my old chair, so I stepped down from the windowsill and headed there. The door to the library was open so I walked in and smelled that old familiar scent of books, heard the creaking of the floors, and saw the twisting, turning rows of shelves. These things made Bridewell feel like home again, like somewhere I belonged.

"Who's visiting?" came a voice from the library office, the messy little room where Grayson spent most of his time mending books and dreaming of strawberry jam.

"It's only me, Grayson," I said. "Just coming to browse and sit a spell before it gets too hot." I'd already seen him at dinner the night before so there was no need for a grand entrance.

Grayson peered around the corner of his office and smiled at me. He was the same plump and happy person I'd left behind the previous summer.

"It's so good to have you back in the library, Alexa. Things have been a mite boring around here in your absence. Maybe you can liven things up a bit." Grayson looked at me sideways, thinking about what he'd said, then added, "Just don't liven things up too much, agreed?" I nodded and smiled, then slowly made my way deeper into the cavernous library.

Walking along the dusty rows of books, my finger scanning the titles, I was struck by the feeling of routine creeping into my bones. The floor still made the same noises as I walked the winding pathway through the library to my favorite chair in the hidden corner, surrounded by towering shelves of books. I tidied the shelves on my way, making for a long meandering journey down many of the aisles. When I arrived at the place where my chair sat I stopped at the windowsill and looked at the wall staring back at me — a blank, unmoving mass of rock brought to life only by the green ivy climbing up and over its top.

My gaze fell on the chair, and I was tempted to move it away and try to open the secret door behind it. I could sneak down into the tunnels below and make my escape into the wild. I could run free. But it would be no use. My father had taken the door's silver key from me and had forbidden me from ever going into the tunnels again. So instead I flopped down in the chair and looked at the books on the shelf next to me. I'd seen them all before and had read and enjoyed many of them. But this time I was looking for one in particular — the one I'd dropped down into the opening behind the secret door last summer, the one called *Adventures at the Border of the Tenth City*. I searched all along the rows of books, moving some out and nudging others in to straighten them perfectly on the shelf. I finally found the book and pulled it out, then settled into the chair and put my feet up on the old wooden box that always served as my footrest.

I flipped open the book and began reading, the breeze outside the window making the ivy leaves along the wall dance and sing as only leaves can do.

And then I heard a different noise. A strange noise. It was a faint, almost unnoticeable, knocking.

*Knock, knock, knock.*

I looked all around, then stood up with the book in

my hand and leaned out the window to listen for the sound again.

*Knock, knock, knock.*

Louder now, but not from outside. I turned and faced the shelves of books and remained very still.

*Knock, knock, knock.*

The book I held slipped out of my hand and fell to the floor with a pop. I remained motionless, not even breathing.

*Knock, knock, knock.*

The sound was coming from behind my chair, from the other side of the secret door.

# CHAPTER 2

# AN UNEXPECTED MESSAGE

I walked back through the library, crisscrossing down several aisles, listening for Grayson to see if he was anywhere nearby. Finding no one, I quickly returned to my chair and began pulling it away from the wall as quietly as I could. Even though I was a year older, I was still as scrawny as ever, hardly a muscle on my bony little arms, and it took all my effort to wrench the chair away from the secret door. I crouched down and listened. Was I hearing things? I started to think I was so desperate for adventure that I'd made up the knocking in my head. But then I heard a soft *click* and the little door swung in slowly on squeaky hinges, revealing only darkness inside.

I held back, too afraid to peer inside. Then a tiny head popped out into the room, accompanied by a high-pitched voice I knew well.

"I was beginning to wonder if you'd leave me hanging here all morning." It was Yipes, dangling on the old ladder that led down into the darkness, a big grin on his small face.

"Yipes!" I said. "What on earth are you doing in there? I can't believe it's you!"

11

He popped out of the tunnel and crouched down next to me behind the chair, then put his finger to his lips.

"*Shhhhhh.* There's no telling who might be milling about the library," he whispered.

"But why are you sneaking around in the old tunnels?" I asked.

He crawled up the back of the chair, scaled one of the tall bookshelves, and disappeared over the top. I could hear him hop from one shelf to another, a quiet, almost imperceptible flitting of his feet. I stayed behind the chair, staring at the shelf he'd disappeared over the top of, wondering where he'd gone and when he might return.

"You can come out now." It was Yipes, sitting on the windowsill behind me. His voice startled me.

"Must you sneak up on me like that? You're worse than Murphy with his slinking around."

"He and I have an agreement," he answered. "It's just too much fun startling you not to try it whenever possible. In any case, Grayson has gone off to the kitchen and the library is empty for the moment. We can talk in peace."

I moved around to the front of the chair and sat down facing the window where Yipes sat on his feet, ready to spring to life should he hear even the smallest disturbance in the library. No matter how many times I saw him, I was always taken aback at how tiny he was. His deeply tanned face was worn and friendly, and he had a smile beneath a pointy little nose that gave away how happy he was to see me.

"It's wonderful to see you, but you shouldn't be sneaking around down there in the tunnels," I said. "They send guards, you know, every hour or so, to make sure people aren't creeping around where they shouldn't be."

Pervis had long ago devised an entrance from within the courtyard, housed in a small stone room, leading down into the tunnels. He'd spent days and days going from chamber to chamber, making sure no one was hiding. The guards knew every way in or out, all of which they had already permanently blocked.

"I don't understand how you even got in there," I continued. "I thought Pervis had sealed off the tunnels from the outside."

Yipes smiled mischievously and leaned closer to me.

"There is still a way for those of us who are small enough." He seemed quite proud of himself, and I was all of a sudden very interested in hearing more about this secret exit and where it might lead.

"There's something important I need to tell you," Yipes went on. He took one last look around, leaning his head from side to side to listen carefully for any noise. "When you were only a few years old, after Renny died, Warvold went on a journey. He was away for quite a long time and nobody knew where he went. When he returned he stopped in to see me, not long after I'd made my home in the wild. He seemed concerned in a way I'd never known him to be, and he gave me something I was to take special care of."

Yipes opened up his vest and dug his little hand inside, fishing around for something. He pulled out a very old and pitiful-looking envelope and held it out to me. The envelope was dirty and torn at the edges, and the writing on the front was smudged with a dried red substance, probably wine from a glass spilled long ago. On the outside were scribbled these eight words:

*For Alexa Daley, one year after I've gone*

I moved into the light of the window and stood next to Yipes. It felt very strange to be holding a message from Warvold. Just hearing his and Renny's names sent shivers of excitement through my bones. But there was another emotion as well. It was odd, but whenever I heard the names of Renny or Warvold, I felt an unusually strong longing to be with them once again.

"Why didn't you give this to me sooner? He's been dead for a year already," I asked.

Yipes shifted back and forth on his feet and looked away from me before answering.

"It's only just been a year since his death," he said. "As you can see by the letter, it says to wait a year. I promise you it was hard not to give it to you sooner. I spent many a night holding it by candlelight trying to read what it says, but the envelope was too thick."

He paused and scratched at his knees.

"In any case, it's in your hand now," he said, "so you had best open it up and see what it says. I have a feeling the time has come for something he intended you to do."

I looked at the envelope, my hand shaking as I held it, and a thousand thoughts ran through my head about what it might contain. I turned it over and carefully tore at the wax seal. Inside was a piece of yellowed paper, folded at the center and ragged on the edges. There was also a smaller envelope enclosed, addressed to my father. I set the smaller envelope aside, opened the first sheet of paper, and began reading aloud.

*Alexa,*

*I have known Yipes for quite some time and he was the only one I could trust with this letter. There is much you need to know but only a little that I can tell you now. If I told you everything I'm afraid you wouldn't have enough courage to undertake what you must, and so I'll only tell you one thing to get you on your way.*

*There is a secret cave in the Dark Hills, beyond anyplace you can see from Bridewell. Within this cave there is something you must retrieve, something very important and very special. This something is for you alone, Alexa, and you must find it. I have taken the liberty of*

*including a letter for your father. Leave it for*
*him, and he won't follow after you. This is a*
*secret journey that he can have no part in. He is*
*aware of certain facts, certain situations, and you*
*can be sure he will understand why you must go*
*into the Dark Hills.*

*Off with you now. Go!*

*Warvold*

Beneath the words was an intricate map. The map led to an entrance I knew nothing of, but beneath the entrance on the map was a squiggly double line clearly marking the place I was to go: *Dark Hills Caves, Secret Far East Chamber.*

I looked up at Yipes, and though I should have been feeling a sense of dread, instead I felt an overwhelming joy at the prospect of adventure. From the grave, Warvold was calling me to do something unexpected and scary, but in my heart I felt as though I'd anticipated just such a development. A big grin spread across my face.

"Yipes, this is incredible," I said. "Will you go with me?"

"I wouldn't have it any other way," he replied.

I could tell he was just as excited as I was at the prospect of what we might find in the Dark Hills.

CHAPTER 3

# THE SECRET CAVE

I ventured back to my room and packed my leather bag with everything I could think of that I might need. On the way back to the library I stopped in the kitchen. It was midmorning and the cooks were taking their break in the smoking room. I went to the large pantry and hoarded all the dried meats and fruits my bag would hold.

When I returned to the library, Grayson was back in his office, mending an especially large book. I peeked in, knowing I couldn't avoid him on my way back to my chair. He turned away from his work and looked up at me.

"Off on a journey, are we?" he said, seeing the bag over my shoulder.

"Just some snacks and books for an afternoon of reading and strolling around town."

"Ahhh. Sounds wonderful. I only wish I could join you. The mending on this book is past due and Silas is scheduled to take it to Ainsworth tonight. I'm afraid I'll be slumped over my desk for some time yet." He turned back to his work and shifted in his chair, his big stomach rubbing against the desk. I was relieved — what if he'd wanted to come with me?

"Happy reading to you," he said, and then I walked away toward the back of the library.

When I arrived back at the chair it was just as I'd left it — back in place, with the secret door shut tight behind it. Yipes was nowhere to be seen, and I began to think again that I'd imagined everything.

I pulled the letter for my father out of my bag and set it on the chair. Then I heard the quiet knocking once more.

*Knock, knock, knock.*

This time I knew it was Yipes, waiting for me on the ladder in the tunnel. I went about the grueling business of pulling the chair out again, and there he was, dangling from the ladder, hiding in case Grayson came to find me. Yipes moved down on the ladder, and I stepped inside, the cool earthen air refreshing on my skin. I took one last look into the library and shut the secret door behind me.

It was darker than I remembered it, the light from the lantern only a faint glow against the smothering blackness all around us. I felt like a tiny firefly, caught all alone in the depths of the night.

"We need to be very quiet," whispered Yipes. "No telling if one of the guards is doing rounds within the tunnels."

I nodded in agreement and we descended to the dirt floor in silence. Yipes led the way as we walked along the tunnel, the light dangling in his tiny hand, shadows thrown along the walls. We walked for some time, twisting and turning into places I'd never been before. As we came upon a sharp turn to the right, Yipes stopped, turned back, and crouched down. Then he blew out the light, and we sat motionless against the tunnel wall.

"What is it?" I whispered. I couldn't see Yipes in the dark, and he made no reply. He only touched my shoulder, moved his hand along my face, and put his fingers over my mouth. A moment later I saw light dancing on the wall, coming from a distance and moving toward us.

My instincts told me to run back before the guard discovered us, but Yipes held me down at my shoulder, as if to tell me we should stay perfectly still. The light came closer, until it was almost on top of us, and I heard the footsteps approaching.

I was fighting the urge to get up and escape as Yipes continued to hold me there, breathless, against the wall. Just about the time I expected to see the guard come around the corner, the light from his lamp began to diminish, and his footsteps became harder to hear, until finally it was all darkness and quiet again.

"Where did he go?" I whispered.

"Another tunnel shoots off to the right, just around the corner. I've been watching the guards as they make their way through the tunnels, and they always turn there, then double back and come this way. We've got only a moment to get across before he returns."

We stood up in the dark and felt along the wall. I followed Yipes as we turned the corner and made our way past the opening where light was moving down the tunnel the guard had entered. Near blind, I stumbled over a rock on the ground, letting out a small gasp as Yipes steadied me and pulled me along more quickly.

"Who's there?" yelled the guard, footsteps sounding toward us.

Yipes hurried me along the floor in the dark, then turned to the left.

"Show yourself!" the guard commanded. But then he went past where we had turned, continuing on in the wrong direction. With the careful silence of cats, Yipes and I moved far enough ahead in our own direction that I began to feel we'd lost the guard in the maze of tunnels.

"That was close," Yipes said, after a time. "But we're almost there now. Just hold my hand — I know the way in the dark."

A few twists and turns later, Yipes stopped and let go of my hand. I couldn't tell where he was, and then a shaft of light appeared near the floor. Yipes had removed the boards from the wall, and with the light from the opening, I found I could see the dimly lit space around me. We had entered a room, surrounded by wood planks on the walls. It looked as though it might have once been sleeping quarters for the escaped convicts who'd hidden in the tunnels before the walls had come down.

"In you go, then," said Yipes. "It's a tight fit, but it's not far to the surface."

Once again, Yipes was pushing me forward. Sometimes

it seemed that forward was the only direction he knew. He'd already pushed me through tunnels and forests. Now he was clearly determined to lead me forward beyond those earlier adventures. He was my friend and I trusted him, so I followed. I moved in front of Yipes and looked into the hole, then I put my arms in front of me as if I were about to dive into a pool of water. It was truly a challenge to move once I was inside, but I managed to slowly inch my way along until my head popped out aboveground in the bright, hot sunlight.

Yipes followed and we found ourselves out in the Dark Hills, the walls of Bridewell standing closer than I'd hoped in the distance. But we were hidden by the thick underbrush, which formed something like a tunnel above the ground, leading away from Bridewell, deeper into the wild.

"That guard might have gone back to bring help," Yipes warned. "They'll be looking for trouble, so we'd best move quickly."

We turned and walked as fast as we could down the hidden pathway. It was hot and cramped as we went, winding our way farther and farther into territory I'd never dreamed I'd be brave enough to venture into. After a long while, Yipes stopped where the pathway split in three directions.

"This is it. This is where the map begins," he said.

I took the map from my bag and laid it flat on the ground. There was indeed a fork on the map with three pathways leading in different directions. The map indicated that we should take the middle fork and follow it until we met with a giant stone somewhere down the way. It was there that we would find an open space and the entrance to the secret cave.

"We're not too far off, maybe a mile," said Yipes. "Let's get on with it. No telling what we'll find when we get there."

About a half hour later we emerged from the confines of the brush, into lands that were more rocky and desolate. We were in a long, skinny ravine, the ground gnarled with deep green brush and sharp, dead trees. It was a dim and gloomy atmosphere. Everything was brittle and hard underfoot. Large, colorless boulders spotted the landscape in every direction.

I sat on the warm ground and spread the map out before me.

"There are rocks all around this place," I said. "But that one is definitely the biggest."

I pointed to a large stone mass protruding from the ground in front of us. It was red and brown and shaped like an enormous nose poking out of the earth.

I wiped my forehead, dripping with sweat, and drank a bit of water from my wineskin. We walked around the rock and the thick brush, looking for an entrance to the cave or a sign that one existed. White cotton clouds crept over the sun, and shadows filled the ravine.

Yipes scampered up the rock and stood at the very tip

of the nose. He seemed to be thinking about the way things looked around him, measuring the dead trees and the brush to see if they were where they ought to be. A moment later he bounded across the rock and jumped down to the ground a few feet across from me.

When he landed it didn't sound like I'd expected it to. I anticipated a hard, solid thud, but instead I heard a hollow emptiness beneath the dirt, as if very little was holding Yipes up. He jumped up and landed on the dirt again, and I had the uneasy feeling that all was not right with this patch of earth. Yipes jumped again and again as he moved away from the rock, and eventually he landed on ground that sounded more like it ought to.

He turned around and faced the rock, crouching down on his knees. At the same time, we both saw with some surprise a small piece of crudely twisted rope, half buried in the dirt. Yipes picked it up and looked at it, then turned and faced me, holding the rope out in his hand.

"You do the honors," he said.

I grabbed the rope and pulled, throwing a dirt-covered wooden door up into the air, bugs and spiders scurrying around its underbelly. A gust of cool, dank air rose from the black hole beneath.

## CHAPTER 4

# JOHN CHRISTOPHER

Yipes and I sat down and let our feet dangle into the hole; the air, though musty, felt refreshing. I ran my hands along the sides of the opening, where the earth was hard. The lower I felt, the cooler the wall became. I let my feet and arms dangle down into the opening for a moment longer, then I felt a spider crawling along my fingers and quickly jerked all my limbs back into the heat of the ravine.

"There's not much choice," said Yipes. "We're going to have to go down in there, and the sooner we do it, the better. At least it won't be as hot as it is out here."

There was no ladder along any of the sides, and though the light poured into the hole, I could not be sure if I was seeing the floor of the tunnel or not. At first I thought the bottom was only seven or eight feet down, a distance I could manage if I jumped in. But then my eyes began to play tricks on me. I wiped the sweat from my face and dropped a rock the size of my fist into the opening while I watched and listened. To my relief it landed quickly and within sight, its gray mass outlined in the shadows less than ten feet below. Yipes jumped first and seemed to have no problem whatsoever with the landing. This gave me the courage I needed to do the same, and though my landing sent me careening across the floor on my hands and knees, we'd made it safely into the secret cave.

I picked up the rock I had tossed into the hole, thinking it might suit me as a weapon should the need arise. The tunnel went in one direction only, and the ceiling was lower than I'd hoped, so low that I had to stoop to manage it. Six steps into this new underground world left me in near-total darkness with Yipes close behind. Something small, probably a field mouse, scurried at my feet as I pushed cobwebs away with my hand. Without thinking, I felt for the dirt ceiling above. As I'd moved along, the tunnel had widened and risen in height, and I realized that I was able to stand upright in the chilly air. In front of me I saw what I expected to see behind me: the light from the opening, looking more like a faraway lamp than light pouring in from outside. I felt along the cold earthen wall and turned back in the other direction. It wasn't until then that I realized the spot we'd gotten ourselves into.

Down the expanse of the tunnel there was a round spot of light — the opening we had come through. I turned and looked again in the direction we were moving and saw the far-off light that looked like a flickering lamp. Then I heard a loud bang off in the distance and turned to see that the round spot of light had disappeared. Someone or something had closed us in.

"That's an unfortunate development," said Yipes.

"We don't have any choice now," I said. "Whatever

Warvold wanted us to find is down here somewhere. I just hope it doesn't have claws and sharp teeth."

A small furry creature brushed against my ankle and I yelped, hopping off the ground, bumping my head against the ceiling, and showering myself with crumbling earth.

"There's something in here with us, Yipes. Something at my feet."

"It's probably just a field mouse or a rat," he replied. "I wouldn't worry too much until you feel a nibble on your toes."

I brushed myself off, then continued walking in the direction of the flickering light, slowly inching my way along in the darkness, my hands held out to gather the cobwebs and feel for obstacles in my path.

"Hello?" I said quietly. "Anyone there?"

"I'm here," Yipes teased.

I smiled in the darkness and asked out loud if anyone besides Yipes was there, but no one answered.

Ten feet away were three wide candles nestled close together on a large stone table. A shadow darted across the wall and my breath was caught in my throat. I leaned flat against the right side of the tunnel and remained still, the cold of the wall gripping the back of my neck. Again I felt the scuffle on my ankle as something moved over my sandals. This time the light from the candles illuminated the floor just enough to make out shapes, and I saw the silhouette of a large rat walking across my left foot. I screamed and kicked the beastly thing across the tunnel. It crashed into the wall with a thud, then scuttled off out of sight.

"Well, come on, then, we haven't got all day. Lots to do and a short time to do it in."

It was a voice I didn't recognize, deep but friendly, coming from somewhere up ahead. Yipes was the first to answer.

"Who are you? What are you doing down here?"

There was a long silence, and then the voice answered.

"My name is John Christopher. Warvold asked me to be here when you arrived. And if that doesn't comfort you, maybe another friend of yours will." The voice was quiet for a moment, and then it spoke again. "That poor beast you've been kicking back and forth in the dark is a rodent that's been driving me half out of my mind down here for hours. He won't stop running around and flitting all over the cave. I believe you both know Murphy."

I came out into the open, and the squirrel ran across the cave in front of me, then leaped into my arms.

"Murphy!" I cried. "What a splendid surprise!"

Yipes walked the rest of the way into the light, and I followed, running my hand over Murphy's soft fur as I went. We found ourselves in a small underground chamber, softly lit by the three large candles.

"It is awfully good to see you again," I whispered to Murphy. "If only I had a Jocasta so we could talk to one another."

"You should get used to stumbling around in the dark," said John. "There will be much of that in the coming days." Candlelight flickered across his face, the glow just enough to make out his bright eyes and the shape of his face. He was a tall man, thin but powerful, and to my surprise he had the letter *C* branded on his forehead. He was a former convict, and I was suddenly very uncomfortable in the confines of the cave.

"I see you've noticed my forehead," said John. "That's good. We might just as well get that out in the open before we do anything more."

I set Murphy down and tapped him on the head, then he scampered a few steps and leaped onto the stone table in the middle of the room. His big furry tail twitched up and down nervously, casting erratic shadows across the walls.

"Murphy!" Yipes cried. "Calm down, will you? You'll give us all a headache." Murphy moved away from the candles, did a backflip, and caught his long tail between two front paws on the way down. He continued to shake and move about nervously, his big black eyes bulging comically, a silly look on his kind little face.

"I don't know what we are to do with him," said John. "The poor thing can't bring himself to sit still. Have you ever spied him sleeping? It's more of the same, twitching and carrying on. I tell you, I don't know how much longer I can stay down here with him. One day is enough to last me a lifetime."

Everyone looked at Murphy, and he sneezed three times in the course of five seconds, all the while trying not to let go of his tail and having quite a time of it. As Yipes tried to calm him down, John began speaking again.

"Where were we?" asked John. "Oh, yes, this letter *C* on my forehead. It's true I was once a convict in the service of Mr. Warvold. But he and I had a special relationship. I was what you might call a petty criminal. I only took what we absolutely needed to survive: a little bread here, a chicken there, the free lodging of a barn or a shed. Warvold saw in me someone he could put to some use, someone he could trust with an important, secret task. It is this task that we must turn our attention to now."

"Why did you close the secret door we entered through?" I blurted out. Come to think of it, I wondered *how* he'd done it as well.

"This is a dangerous place you've stumbled into. You never know who or what might be lurking about in the Dark Hills, what might have found its way down here had I not sealed us in."

"Yes, but how did you close it from way back here?" I asked. I wasn't sure I trusted John Christopher yet.

"Let's just say there is more than one way into this room, and I was aware of your arrival when you opened the door to get in."

Murphy let go of his tail, and it darted up and down again, casting shadows all over the room.

"Murphy!" yelled Yipes. This time the squirrel jumped off the table and back into my arms, burying its head next to my elbow. There was a deep silence in the room. I watched in disbelief as John leaned over and blew out the candles, leaving us in complete darkness.

There was no protection now.

# CHAPTER 5

# WHAT WARVOLD LEFT BEHIND

A cold blackness enveloped the space. I was afraid, and I stepped back for a wall to lean against while I called into the darkness for Yipes. Murphy became restless in my arms and darted up to my shoulder, where he sat flicking his tail against the back of my head. I turned to look at him, my nose touching his, but I could not make out his face.

"Take my hand," said John. "Come on, reach out and take it. We've very little time, and certainly none to be wasted on meandering about like the blind."

I felt uneasy about putting my hand in his. I hardly knew him at all and he was much bigger than I was. In the dark of the cave I felt my hands shaking, and I felt trapped, as though I had no choice but to do as I was told.

I kept one hand on the wall and reached out in the air of the cave with the other. When I touched John's hand I realized how comparatively small mine was. The coarse texture of his skin felt like an old knotted rope. I held tight to his hand, and he pulled me along the wall of the cave until I was unclear where we were.

"Sit down, Alexa," he said. I felt the cool dirt floor

31

beneath me with my free hand and slowly sat down. Murphy remained on my shoulder, holding my thick hair between his front paws and shivering with fright. Yipes was somewhere in the room, but he was quiet, so I couldn't be sure where he was or what he was doing.

I sat in the black cave only a moment longer, and I listened as the sound of rock sliding against rock came from a short distance away. Then, miraculously, the cave was aglow in watery light, much brighter than the candlelight had been. As the sound of sliding rock persisted, a kaleidoscope of fiery colors ran liquid all around us. I crawled over to the source as Murphy scampered onto my back, and I peered over the edge of a large boulder. Its top was flat, and the inside had been cut into a bowl. Within the bowl lay a foot of water, and at the bottom sat a glowing stone, pulsating red and yellow like embers in a fire.

"A Jocasta," I whispered.

"The last one," said John, his face aglow as he gazed over the edge of the pool looking as though he'd found the greatest of long-lost treasures.

"It was placed here years ago under Warvold's direction," he continued. "The cave entrance used to be there, but it was easily seen, so he covered it up." John pointed to a pile of rocks a few feet away, obscuring what had clearly been an opening at one time.

"We are well past where the convicts dug their tunnels near Bridewell. They never came out so far into the

Dark Hills. At least most of them didn't." Here John paused, reached over, and tapped Murphy on the head. "Warvold appointed me the task of digging the short tunnel that leads to this cave, as well as blocking the old entrance. It was me who chose the soft stone that would hold the last of the Jocastas, chiseled out its middle, and found a slab of rock that would perfectly cover the top of the secret pool. It was a task that required many years, as you might imagine."

Yipes leaned over the edge of the pool and looked into the water, the glow of the Jocasta shimmering across his face. He had a deep longing in his face, as though he'd found something he was sure no longer existed. It would take him but a moment to snatch it in his miniature hands.

"This stone was appointed for you, Alexa," said John. Yipes looked at me and nodded his agreement with a smile. "We don't know why this is so, but it's what Warvold told me to tell you both. There is something more to this stone, something more than all the rest."

All of this had been done for me? All the careful planning and work to protect this one stone. It was hard to imagine. Warvold had trusted John Christopher with quite a lot, and suddenly I felt I could trust him as well.

"If you don't take it soon, Murphy's head will explode," said Yipes. "He must be very excited to talk with you."

The last Jocasta. Yipes and I had been back to the glowing pool upon Mount Norwood many times hoping to find one. And all this time one had been waiting, hidden by Warvold in the cave. Murphy began scratching at my back, and I reached down into the clear, cold water. I put my fingers around the smooth, plum-sized stone and pulled it out into the air.

"Murphy the brave, at your disposal!" said the squirrel on my back.

The magic of the Jocastas remained. What followed were a few minutes of chatter between old friends, mostly catching up on where we had been and what we had been doing. Murphy had been sitting down to a nice walnut for supper when John came calling.

"John has lived in the wild since before the walls went up, and he visited the glowing pool quite a long time before you did," Murphy told me.

John opened a leather pouch around his neck and removed a glowing blue stone.

"It's not the last stone, but it will do," said John. We both looked at Yipes and wished he could go back in time and have his own Jocasta restored. But he seemed perfectly content to have us do the translating for him.

"I'm just happy to be a part of the adventure," he said.

"There's no more time to waste yapping in the cave," John broke in. "You two can talk all you want aboveground."

34

By the light of the Jocastas we walked the length of the tunnel, John in front.

"How did you know we would arrive here today?" I asked our guide.

John laughed out loud.

"You can't imagine how many times I wanted to tell Yipes to give you the letter. It's been my sole duty to watch and wait for him to deliver it to you. The boredom was excruciating. As soon as he went off to get you, I gathered Murphy and another friend as Warvold had instructed and came straight here. We've been waiting for you since last night."

We arrived where the secret door had been thrown shut. I had brought my first Jocasta with me, now dull and lifeless in its pouch around my neck. John instructed me to remove the old stone and place the new Jocasta inside. This command I obeyed, and when John placed his Jocasta back in its hiding place, all was dark once more.

I heard a pop above my head, the sound of a stone hitting against the bottom of the wood door. A moment later the door flew open and stinging bright light enveloped the space. I had to shield my eyes before looking up through the opening. A silhouette peered over the edge, but it wasn't that of a person.

"She's grown quite a lot. Not the little girl she once was." It was a gentle growling of words, the mystic voice of a wolf, the outline of its huge head glaring down upon me.

"That she has," said John, pulling a ladder from the shadows in the corner and placing it against the wall of the tunnel.

"Darius, is that you?" I asked as I scampered onto the edge of the opening, and Murphy jumped free of my shoulder.

"I'm afraid his adventuring days are over, so you'll have to settle for the likes of me." It was Odessa, Darius's wife. She was every bit the hulking figure Darius was, with piercing blue eyes and massive white teeth. She was a powerful creature, and even though I knew instinctively that she was my ally, her presence was so frightening I had trouble standing next to her. Not so for Murphy, who had already leaped onto Odessa's back and was busy jumping up and down and squeaking for no particular reason. (Odessa seemed not to care.)

Yipes came up the ladder and stood beside me, then John slammed the door shut and sealed off the cave below. As we stood in the ravine, the wind began to blow, and a hawk drifted down to earth and sat upon Yipes's shoulder.

"I was wondering when you would return, you rascal. Out hunting again, are we?" said Yipes. "And stop looking at Murphy like that. He's not a meal, he's a member of our party." Murphy clung tightly to Odessa's fur, and his tiny eyes were wide and dark.

Thus the group was assembled: Yipes, John Christopher, Murphy, Odessa the wolf, the hawk (named Squire), and me. It was a strange assortment of animals

36

and humans, and it struck me then that Warvold saw far beyond what the eye beholds in its view of a creature. For who would think to leave this world entrusting a grand unfinished quest to a mere child, a former convict, a grown man no larger than a five-year-old boy, and an odd assortment of animals?

John had prepared well. There were three leather packs, one large and two small, along with a supply of water held within four good-sized wineskins. The wineskins were laced together, two on each side, and the whole water supply was set upon Odessa's back and secured around her waist and neck. The skins held a gallon or more of water each, but dangling at Odessa's enormous sides they seemed more than manageable. She would have no trouble with her duty.

I found my pack to be quite heavy and hot against my sweating back. Murphy added a pound or two by making his home in the leather where the drawstring was pulled behind my head. Squire was off again, flying in front of us in the clouds, and my two human companions appeared ready to depart.

"Just one more thing, Alexa," said Yipes as he pulled a small magnifying glass from a pocket in his vest. "You know the stones are inscribed with a message for the person they choose. Shall we take a look and see?"

I had a strange, uncertain feeling about the stone now in my hand, and for reasons I can't explain, I didn't want to know what it might say.

"I think I'll wait, if you don't mind," I said.

Yipes puzzled over my decision, shrugged, and began gathering the last of his things. When he was ready he ran his fingers over his mustache and looked around at the group of us.

"Now what?" he asked, and we all looked at John, hoping he had some idea what we were meant to do next.

## CHAPTER 6

# THE BLACK SWARM

Standing in the open space of the Dark Hills was uncomfortable, with the sun beating down and a growing fear that someone might come looking for us.

"Yipes," I said, "do you think that guard would come all the way out here trying to find us?"

Yipes thought a moment and replied, "I don't imagine so. They're probably busy searching through the tunnels. They won't think we've gotten so far out into the Dark Hills."

We were all standing together, wondering what we should do now that I'd accomplished the task Warvold had set out for me in his letter.

"I don't understand," I said. "Why would Warvold send me here to get the last stone and then leave no other instructions? Do you suppose he just wanted me to have it?"

John and Murphy exchanged glances, and then John knelt down and inspected his pack to be sure everything was secure.

"There are a few things I know," he said. "Things that Warvold shared with me over the years — clues to why we're here and where we're meant to go."

He looked up at us and wiped his brow with the back of his hand. Then he spoke.

"Somewhere past the Dark Hills lies the Valley of Thorns. At the end of the valley is a lake of unusual depth and darkness, and at its distant shore sits the Dark Tower."

This sounded like the start of one of Warvold's spooky stories. John took a long breath and continued.

"Though no one from Bridewell Common ever travels there, more than once Warvold journeyed to the Dark Tower and the poor town it rules. He spoke to me in whispers of these places and their history. There is more I can tell you about it as we make our way, but we can't stay here any longer. There are unseen dangers in this place."

He rose once again and threw his pack over his shoulder, then pointed deeper into the Dark Hills.

"What I can tell you right now is this: We must travel beyond the Valley of Thorns, to the places where Warvold ventured. Only there will we find the answers we're looking for."

For the first time I began to wonder what I'd gotten myself into. This sounded far too dangerous for a girl of thirteen, especially without the permission of her parents.

"Are you sure about this?" I asked. "I can't imagine what my father would say if he were to find out I'd gone off so far from home. He'd be furious." But even as I said it I remembered the letter from Warvold. *This is a secret journey that he can have no part in. He is aware of certain facts, certain situations, and you can be sure he will understand why you must go into the Dark Hills.*

"It's your decision, Alexa," said John. "Either way, we have to be moving along. We can't stay here any longer."

My hand instinctively went to the leather pouch around my neck, and I felt the Jocasta hidden inside. *The last Jocasta.* It was in my possession, and Warvold wanted it taken somewhere for some purpose. If I returned to Bridewell, that something would be left unfinished, with terrible consequences I couldn't begin to understand.

"Lead the way," I said to John.

It wasn't long before we all realized why the Dark Hills was a place that, once visited, was rarely returned to with fond memories. Only an hour into our journey, we were forced to stop as the sun pounded us with crippling heat. I felt most sorry for Odessa and Murphy, who was out of my pack and walking now; covered with thick fur, they were almost certainly suffering from exhaustion. But neither of them complained, and though our conversations lagged, they continued on in good spirits.

The real problem with the Dark Hills was the lack of shelter. The farther we traveled, the more desolate the terrain became. Other than the occasional boulder casting a droplet of shade, it was a dead stretch of dry dirt and gnarly underbrush that cut and grabbed at your legs like sharp claws. Amid all of this uninhabited bleakness we found a rather large rock, and this we sat next to, opposite the sun. The ground had been heating up all day, as had the rock, and these facts, as well as the meager shade the rock provided, gave our moment of rest a sense of hopelessness. We did enjoy a drink of water and a bite of dried fruit, and these were taken with great pleasure and a measure of relief. But the reality of the situation was beginning to set in: Our adventure would be hard and dangerous work that would push us beyond our limits.

"How are you holding up, Alexa?" Odessa asked. "This is difficult terrain on four feet — I can't imagine how hard it must be on two."

I was reminded of the journey I'd taken up Mount Norwood when I'd first met Yipes, how that journey had ended at the glowing pool with my feet blistered and sore.

"I think I'll manage," I answered. "I only wish it wasn't so very hot."

"We're nearing sunset," said Yipes. "Things will cool down soon."

John looked at the lot of us, weary from the day's travel.

"Have any of you heard of something they call the black swarm?" he asked.

We all looked at one another, wondering what he was talking about. It was clear we'd never heard of such a thing.

"We have a ways to go before we reach shelter," he continued. "I've been out past here before, and there is a place we must find."

John paused and took a quick drink from one of our wineskins of water.

"I haven't been there for a very long time, but I think we can reach it by nightfall. Best we do — the swarm comes out at night."

"John," Yipes began, nervous fear growing in his voice, "what's the black swarm?"

John took one more drink before answering.

"Bats," he said. "But not the kind that feed on bugs. These bats stay together in a giant, swirling mass, and they look for prey to devour. I've only seen them once, from a distance, but Warvold was familiar with them. If they find us, our journey will come to a quick end."

We were all on our feet then, ready to make for shelter before nightfall without another word of encouragement from John.

The next two hours were hard fought against the elements. Though my body was drenched in sweat and my back was sore, it was my ankles that really began to bother me. I had brushed against countless sharp, dry bushes and thistles. My legs burned and itched from my knees all the way down to my feet, and within my sandals, dirt and tiny stones grated and stung as I walked.

Night was falling as we arrived at a large dead tree, broken in the middle and charred from a past fire, its top section fallen against a grouping of fat red stones.

Murphy hopped to the top of the broken tree, scanning the horizon for Squire, who we hadn't seen for over an hour. She was the aloof one of the group, partly due to her natural tendencies as a hawk, but probably more because none of us could talk with her. For whatever reason, the Jocastas had no effect with birds.

"Over here," said John. He had gone around the other side of the tree and was crouching in the dirt. I came around the corner and bent down next to him. There on the ground was a large rock, John's hand running along its smooth surface. I was beginning to have trouble seeing as the night crept in.

I heard Squire shriek from the air, a long way off. I turned to look for her, but she was lost in the darkening sky.

"Squire has rejoined us," said Murphy, and he jumped off the tree onto Odessa's back, shivering with fright.

"That's not Squire," said Yipes. "That's something else."

John stood and scanned the horizon, and then he spoke a single word that sent a chill down my spine.

"Bats."

# CHAPTER 7
# CLUES IN THE DARKNESS

"Everyone, against the rock!" John shouted. He was leaning all his weight into the large stone he'd been touching. It was tilting up off the ground a few inches, then crashing back down with a thud.

Yipes was the first to join him, then Odessa placed her head against the stone, pushing with her legs. A moment later the three of them had the large stone rolled over on its side, revealing the entrance to an underground space. It looked awfully dark and small from where I was standing.

The bats shrieked once more, and I turned toward the sound. But in the darkness of night I could not make out shapes in the air. They were closer — close enough to see us if we didn't hide quickly.

"In you go," said John, looking at me.

"When was the last time you were down there?" I asked. "Maybe something crawled in, and it's waiting for the first of us to step inside." I was reminded of the first time I'd gone into the tunnels in Bridewell, how it felt like walking into the mouth of a giant.

Murphy scampered past me and down into the space, then squeaked from inside.

"It's no problem," he said. "Just a barren space, nothing much to look at."

The shrieking of the bats was very close, and I was sure anything would be better than being chewed apart by them. I descended, and the others followed quickly behind me.

I found that I could not stand upright, so I crouched down against a wall, where Murphy jumped into my lap. At the bottom of the small opening to the space was another large stone, this one rounder in its shape than the other had been. John immediately put his shoulder against the stone and began rolling it in front of the opening. As it covered the last of the entrance I could hear the flapping of leathery wings and the deafening sound of bats flying in a swarm overhead. It sounded as though some of them were beating their wings against the other side of the rock, swirling around in the space just above us. And then they were gone, the sound of them nothing but a shrill whisper. I realized how very dark it was.

Everyone remained quiet, still afraid a lone bat was hanging behind the stone, waiting to hear us so it might chase after the swarm and bring it back. But there was nothing, only the sound of our breathing and the flit of Murphy's tail as he tried to keep still.

I heard John fumbling for something, and then the room was aglow with soft blue light, cast from the Jocasta he held in his hand. He held the light out in front of him, and I was able to see for the first time the place where we'd arrived.

It was a small, low, covered room without furnishings of any kind. There were, however, two oddities I immediately spied — a wooden cup, chipped and scuffed, resting atop a neatly folded blanket. These items sat alone in the middle of the room.

"We can talk now. They've passed on," said John. I could see Yipes as I crawled over next to the cup and the blanket and sat down. He, Odessa, and Murphy were the only ones who could stand upright in the room, and Odessa just barely.

"This is my kind of place," Yipes joked. "Cozy, and the ceiling is just the right height."

He smiled and looked around the room happily, the watery blue light from the stone dancing in his eyes.

"We'll have to stay here for the night," said John. "I can move the stone back a little to let in fresh air, but only after we've put the Jocasta away."

Yipes removed the wineskins from Odessa's back, and John began setting out nuts and fruit and dried meat. I took the old cup that was sitting on the blanket in my

48

hand and turned it, wondering who might have left it behind.

"Warvold journeyed here," said John. "More than once is my guess. He told me of this place a long while ago. I'm a bit surprised I was able to lead us here without too much trouble."

Sometime in the distant past, Warvold had drunk from this cup. He'd been here, sitting in this very spot, hiding from the black swarm just as we were.

I took the corner of the folded blanket and began wiping the dust from the inside of the cup.

"What's this?" asked Murphy. He'd been scampering all around the room, running up and down the walls, sniffing everywhere he went. He'd arrived at the blanket, his nose beneath where I'd lifted the corner to clean the cup. When he emerged he held pieces of paper between his teeth. I snatched them out of his mouth and set down the cup.

It was a marvelous discovery, and everyone gathered closer to see them, excited about what the pages might contain. I flipped the pages over in my hands and realized what a treasure Murphy had found.

"This is Warvold's writing!" I cried out. Murphy could hardly contain himself, flipping and scuffling all around. There were five pages, covered in words on both sides, all in Warvold's familiar scrawl.

John held his Jocasta closer and everyone crowded

together. Odessa lay down next to me, gnawing on a chunk of dried meat, and Murphy jumped onto her back.

I filled the wooden cup with water and took a long drink, then cleared my throat and read what the pages said so everyone could hear.

CHAPTER 8

# CASTALİA

*"There is only one other person, alive or dead, who I've told about this secret place. I made this shelter many years ago, and I've taken refuge here often as I've traveled between the far reaches of The Land of Elyon. I fear this is the last time I will ever see these walls, and there are things I must write down, should I meet unexpectedly with my demise.*

*John Christopher, I do hope you've managed to find this letter. More important, I hope you have Alexa with you and that she carries the last stone.*

*Have patience as I tell you a brief history of the places beyond the Valley of Thorns."*

I looked at the faces glowing blue all around me. Everyone had stopped eating, even Odessa.

"This ought to be interesting," said Yipes. Then he tossed a nut into his mouth and leaned forward like a child about to hear a wonderful story. I drank again from the old wooden cup and began reading once more.

*"Some three hundred years ago there arose a small king-dom at the edge of a wide lake. The lake they called Castalia, and soon after, the kingdom itself took the same name.*

*The Castalians thrived for a hundred years. The water*

*from the lake fed their crops, and their numbers grew until many thousands lived along the shore. But then the Castalians had an unfortunate bit of bad luck.*

*They were visited by a man named Victor Grindall. Though of average size and modest appearance himself, he had with him a band of a hundred men very large in stature, more than twice the size of anyone in Castalia.*

*The Castalians were a timid people, never having been bothered by anyone, and they knew little of weapons or war. Grindall's men, though pleasant in appearance, were intimidating because of their size. Grindall gave the Castalians a choice: either make him their ruler or his giants would overrun the city and take it by force.*

*Many years later, the descendants of Grindall and the giants remain, and even now Castalia lies in the hands of an evil man and the dark forces that guide him."*

I looked up, confused by the strange story Warvold had begun.

"Warvold was a teller of tall tales," I said, trying to lighten my own mood. "This sounds like something he would write."

But even as I said it, I somehow got the feeling that this story was not like the others.

"Would you like me to finish reading it?" asked Yipes. "Whether it's true or not, I want to know what happens!" He reached out his hand and I gave him the pages. Then I took the wooden cup in both hands and held it, running my thumb along the chipped edge, hoping to feel Warvold's presence in the room.

Yipes continued on at a merry pace, his high voice bouncing off the walls.

"Not so long ago, two sisters lived in Castalia. The elder was named Catherine and her younger sister was named Laura. The two of them lived in secret among the poor of Castalia, during the ninth reign of Grindall. Few can tell of how they came to live in hiding and what they discovered in the dead of night, but I will tell you a little of the story.

The girls were orphans. Catherine was thirteen and Laura was eleven, and they were forced to take care of each other and find food and shelter amid the poverty of the town square. Castalia had long since become a sprawling peasant village. The Dark Tower loomed high above — an ominous, dark spire in which generation after generation of Grindall men had forged their cruelest intentions.

The girls were determined to escape Castalia and find a new home, even though the gates were guarded by giants. Catherine was a crafty girl, always watching, and she discovered a way out. Together the sisters hid within the confines of a garbage cart and were rolled through the gate and out of the city to the dumping grounds.

The girls found themselves in a space overgrown with trees and brush, and most of the structures around them had walls that had fallen in and were now filled with rubbish. A terrible smell haunted the air. They had been dumped into an area once inhabited by Castalians but now used as the place where all the refuse was thrown. This place had long been called the City of Dogs, because large packs of wild dogs roamed there, living off what they could find among the mire in which the girls now found themselves.

They came upon an old, vine-covered clock tower — a stone relic at the corner of a forgotten street near the edge of the dump — that had long since been left in ruin. The clock tower was to become their home.

On that first night they remained on the ground floor, too afraid to climb the ladder on the wall and push on the door in the ceiling. But the next morning, hungry and bored, the girls climbed the seven steps and pushed on the wooden door that led to the clock tower. The door was blocked and would not move, and though I was not there and only heard the story secondhand, it was told to me that at precisely this moment a pack of wild dogs began sniffing around the base of the old structure, growling menacingly at the smell of new inhabitants."

"Slow down, Yipes," said John. "I can hardly make out what you're saying."

Yipes was breathless, reading at a frantic pace, overcome with anticipation as the story became more and more perilous. He stopped and held the pages out to me.

"You'd better finish it, Alexa," he said. "I won't be able to stop myself from racing to the end. But don't go *too* slowly, all right?"

I nodded and took the pages in my hand, scanning them until I found the place where Yipes had been interrupted. I was frightened of where the story might lead, but I was also terribly curious about a great many things. What would happen to Catherine and Laura? Why did Warvold leave a note about them? Who were they? And what of these giants and Victor Grindall — were they real or imagined?

I steadied my shaking hands, took a deep breath, and read on.

*"The girls looked down from their perch on the ladder and realized the stone they had removed to enter the building had not been replaced. The wild dogs were coming in, a pack of them, frothing and snarling as they approached the ladder. And then something very curious happened.*

*The door at the top of the ladder opened.*

*Seeing no other choice, Catherine and Laura scampered inside and stood against the wall. There was only a faint light in the space, but it was clear that something was hiding there. A match was struck and a fat old candle was lit in a corner. A creature sat hunched against the wall, arms folded around bent knees.*

*It was a giant."*

# CHAPTER 9
# WHAT THE GIANT TOLD

We had read half of what Warvold wrote, the room turning stale from lack of fresh air. But that didn't matter. We were all caught up in the story.

"Wait just a moment while I let in a bit of air," said John.

He crawled over to the stone, unable to stand upright in the room, and then he put his Jocasta back inside its leather pouch.

The room was suddenly dark, so dark that I couldn't see the pages in my hand as I heard the rock move against the opening. Warm air crept slowly into the room, whipping tiny specks of dust on a soft evening breeze. We sat silent in the darkness, waiting for the light of the Jocasta to return.

John Christopher was as curious as we were to finish the story Warvold had left for us, and we didn't wait long to hear the stone rolling back and see the room aglow once more in blue light.

"Only a few pages to go," I said, flipping the papers in my hand. "Shall I continue?" Everyone nodded eagerly, and my voice filled the room with the rest of Warvold's tale.

"And here we find ourselves before a creature with knowledge of things no peasant of Castalia or ruler of Bridewell could know. On that first evening, Catherine, Laura, and the giant became acquainted, and in the days that followed, the giant told them a great many secrets about himself, his race, and the history of the Grindalls. What I am going to tell you now will draw you into a conflict from which you cannot turn. Your enemy, who prowls as close as the Valley of Thorns, will become clear as crystal on this very night.

When Elyon created the world and the human race he also created something else — a hundred powerful beings he called Seraphs. These beings were made to protect The Land of Elyon from within the realm of the Tenth City, a secret place where Elyon made his home and everything could be seen. While the Seraphs were created to oversee the human race, they were forbidden to ever leave the Tenth City.

One of the Seraphs was called Abaddon, and he was more powerful than all the rest. Abaddon was overcome with jealousy and wanted to rule The Land of Elyon. In secret, he convinced the Seraphs that they must enter the realm of men and women to protect them. When the Seraphs arrived in The Land of Elyon they took the form of giants, larger than normal men, stronger, and still with some lingering powers.

When Elyon discovered what the Seraphs had done, he was enraged and he banished them from the Tenth City forever. Abaddon, his power growing uncontrollable, was harder to contain than the other ninety-nine. A great battle ensued between Elyon and Abaddon, and in the end Abaddon was chained down in a great pit at the edge of the Tenth City.

Elyon uses a great deal of his own strength to keep Abaddon in the pit. Still, even though Abaddon cannot leave the pit, he is able to assert his will in various ways. He is able to corrupt men from afar, encouraging their evil for his purposes. And then there are the bats. Innocently present in the pit when Abaddon arrived, they are now poisoned by his will, swarming The Land of Elyon.

Abaddon wants to destroy The Land of Elyon along with the Tenth City, so he can rule everything and drive Elyon away.

To do this, Abaddon must prey on the evil and the weak, using them to achieve his goals. Victor Grindall is the most powerful man to have fallen under Abaddon's spell. Abaddon can bend Grindall's will to do his bidding.

In this case, he is using Grindall to search for the stones.

Where, you may ask, do the stones come from? There once was a place in The Land of Elyon that no longer exists, a place that was only known by Elyon and the Seraphs. This was a magical place, where creation began and the first voices were heard. Long ago there was only one language between the animals and humans, and even Elyon's voice could be heard and understood by a few. Unable to return to the Tenth City, it was in this place that the Seraphs first made their home, hidden from people.

This place was supposed to be a secret. But Abaddon used Grindall to make his way there, saying things the Seraphs seemed to understand. Something about Grindall made them follow. Little did they know it was the voice of Abaddon, calling them from the pit to do his bidding.

Through Grindall, Abaddon instructed the giants to gather the stones that lay in a pool in this secret place, stones that would contain the power to hear the original language of Elyon. And then the Seraphs left, following the only voice that sounded anything like home. And Victor Grindall led them to Castalia.

But Abaddon was deceived, for some of the stones were enchanted by Elyon so that they might only fall into the hands of those he chose."

"There's only one more page," I said. Everyone in the room looked as confused and amazed as I felt.

"Read the last of it, Alexa," said John. "I have a feeling we haven't heard the most important part yet."

Somehow I felt the same, like something dreadful was about to happen. I held the last page closer to the light of the Jocasta and started reading.

"Two hundred years after the first Grindall was dead and gone, Armon the giant was appointed keeper of the stones. The line of Grindall was in its ninth reign, and the remaining stones were kept in a pool in the deepest part of the Dark Tower, in the darkest corner of the dungeon, where Armon guarded them.

Day after day, Armon watched the stones as they sat quietly in a pool of water, until one day a single stone began glowing faintly. Overcome with curiosity, Armon picked up the stone and for a brief moment heard the forgotten sound of Elyon's voice, distant but clear, coming from the Tenth City. From that moment on, Armon was compelled to protect the remaining stones, to remove them, and to leave Castalia. He escaped into the City of Dogs, hid in the clock tower, and was discovered by Catherine and Laura.

When Armon touched the stone, Abaddon at last realized what Elyon had done. He understood that the remaining stones had the power to destroy him if they were carried to those Elyon had chosen. And so Abaddon infected the reigning Grindall with all his might, giving him an unquenchable thirst for the stones.

We find ourselves now in the depth of the tenth reign of Grindall, and if things have gone as I've hoped, Alexa holds the very last of the stones. From the beginning Elyon has chosen her, and he has left the fate of the world in her hands.

It falls to Alexa now to defeat Abaddon."

# CHAPTER 10

# JOURNEY ACROSS THE DARK HILLS

As you might imagine, I was speechless. I sat silently contemplating what it all meant. If this tale was true then I held the last Jocasta, and this band of misfits I'd surrounded myself with was all I had to help me. It struck me then that this was the same sort of group that had managed to bring down the walls around my kingdom and save Bridewell from the evil plot set against it. John Christopher, Yipes, Murphy, Odessa, and Squire — whatever trouble I'd fallen into, I had to believe these companions would protect and help me to the end. As I looked around at the faces before me I was comforted — even excited — to walk the paths old Warvold had tread, into places I could only imagine. I smiled.

"BOO!" I yelled.

Yipes jumped up so fast he bumped his head on the ceiling, while Murphy spun and rolled off Odessa's back, landed on his feet, and scampered into a corner of the room. John and Odessa only flinched and remained where they were.

"Why must you do things like that?" pleaded Yipes. "You've scared poor Murphy half out of his wits."

I chuckled, then John joined in, and pretty soon we were all laughing, our nervous energy released into the small room. When everyone became calm and quiet again, I showed the back of the last page of Warvold's notes.

"There's another map here," I said. "It looks as though it will be our guide for the next few days."

It was a crude drawing of markers and lines with a title scribbled across the top that read *Across the Dark Hills to the Valley of Thorns — route void of BATS*.

"That's encouraging," said Murphy from his new perch atop my shoulder. Squirrels have surprisingly sharp claws, and he was digging in more than usual.

"You're holding on a bit tight, Murphy," I said. "Not scared, are you?"

Murphy loosened his grip and put his wet nose in my ear, something he did when he'd had enough of my pestering.

"Best to get some rest," said John. "By the looks of that map, we've got at least three days of travel through harsh lands in front of us. We should get some sleep while we have the safety of this room."

Everyone seemed to agree. The Jocasta was put away and the rock rolled back just enough to let in a trickle of fresh air again. Before long I was the only one awake. The deep darkness of the room scared me. To comfort myself I thought about my desk back home in Lathbury — its top the color of walnut shells, the aged wood somehow soft and hard at the same time, the smell of old books all around me. I rolled onto my side and held Murphy against my chest with one arm, his slight breathing and warm coat comforting me. It wasn't long before I, too, was fast asleep like the rest.

The predawn hours were colder than expected, and everyone woke early the next morning. We packed our few belongings quickly and began walking north, the presence of the sun known only by a delicate tint of orange along the horizon. Right away I felt the first burning scratches of dried brush along my legs, the dusty earth beneath my feet. Murphy sat on my pack, nibbling on a few nuts while I ate from a handful of dried apples and figs.

For the next three days we followed the map, ever wary of intruders, an endless trek into barren lands. I could only guess, but by the end of the fourth day I thought we must have been a hundred miles from Bridewell, miles that would have been impossible to cross on horseback with the many crevices and climbs. As the sun was setting I looked back toward where we'd come and realized with some astonishment how far away from home I was.

"We should keep moving as best we can until night falls," said Yipes. "We're nearing the end of the map, but we're also running low on food and water."

I'd forgotten how determined Yipes could be when he set his mind to something. By the look of the map we would arrive at the edge of the Valley of Thorns sometime the next day. We were all terribly curious what the Valley of Thorns was, but the mere sound of it worried me.

"The days get easier for me as we go," said Odessa. "Less water is less for me to carry — that and Murphy every now and then, but he's as light as a feather."

The evening light passed quietly as the heat let go of its grip on the land. Squire rejoined us, alighting on John's pack and looking around nervously for field mice she might have the good fortune to discover. John took a piece of dried meat from a small pocket on the side of his tunic and held it behind his head. Squire immediately snapped it away and ripped it into small bits between her claws and her beak. Not long after that she flew off again. I made a game with Murphy of trying to track where Squire had gone, until she flew into the horizon and we both lost her.

Soon after, we fell into a conversation about the merits of having a body covered with hair. It became quite lively, the two animals extolling a lengthy list of reasons why hair upon one's body was to be envied and insisting that a hairless beast walking upright on two feet was a disgusting thing indeed, a sight which had been largely spared them by the use of clothing. Yipes, John, and I were victorious in the end, but only because the oppressive heat emphasized the inherent problem of having a coat you could never take off.

When I looked up again the sun was only a far-off sliver, and we found a clearing surrounded by a thicket to shelter us for the night. We were now only hours from the Valley of Thorns, and everyone was concerned about what we might encounter there.

"The sooner we get to the Valley of Thorns, the sooner we can find out what all this means," said John. "The best we can do now is rest and rise early. By tomorrow afternoon we'll be there."

"I wonder what became of the girls," I said, already lying down with my head resting on my pack.

"Catherine and Laura," I whispered, already drifting off to sleep, exhausted from the long day. "I wonder where they went, or if we'll ever find out." I tried to stay awake and think more about the mystery, but a moment more and I fell into a deep sleep.

Sometime later, in the full of night, I was awakened by Odessa. She had been guarding the camp for several hours, and it was my turn to do the same. The night air had gone cold and I shivered in my effort to sit up, placing my arms around my knees.

"All's quiet?" I whispered.

"Squire flew in an hour ago and startled me, but she's resting by Yipes now," the wolf answered. "Otherwise it's been silent but for John. He's more restless than usual tonight, waking often and looking around to see if I am still at my duty."

I got up and walked to the edge of our camp, looking out across what remained of the Dark Hills. So bleak, so desolate. Even in the night I clearly understood its awful barrenness. I looked back and saw that Odessa had curled up next to John, the two of them whispering. And then I saw Murphy sneak slowly across the camp and curl into a ball of fur at John's feet. The hours of my watch drifted by, filled with thoughts of Castalia and all its strange wonders, until the first orange glow of morning touched our camp and all at once everyone was stirring, wakeful, slowly preparing their things for our final walk on the ground of the Dark Hills.

# CHAPTER 11

# MY SPYGLASS GETS SOME USE

"Someone is near," said John.

"What do you mean?" asked Odessa, sniffing at the air to catch an unknown scent. But John continued ahead without offering an answer. When I probed him further he turned and addressed all of us at once.

"There's something not right about this place. It's like the feeling I have when it's dark outside and I think maybe there is someone watching me. And then I hear a twig snap and my heart jumps. That's the feeling I've had all morning."

"What do you suppose it is, John?" Yipes asked. His voice expressed the concern we were all feeling.

John shrugged, turned, and began walking again. "I haven't the slightest idea."

We had been walking all morning, mostly in silence, and the anxiety we felt was only heightened by what John had said. I wished then that John had kept his feelings to himself. But he hadn't, and I was left to imagine all manner of beastly monsters overtaking us in the gloom of the Dark Hills.

We had been moving in the direction of a great hill

for some time, and in due course we found ourselves at its edge in a dry ravine. Though I would not call it a mountain, the hill before us was both steep and of great length from side to side, running off at both ends well beyond where we could see. Since we couldn't see a way to get around it, we knew we'd have to go over the top. We thought it best to stop and review the map while we indulged in a few minutes of rest before starting the climb.

I looked across the parched earth and watched as Murphy cleaned between his paws and ran his little forelegs over his head and back again. Standing as I was between Yipes and John, it struck me how filthy they were. Stubble marked their faces and dirty hair hung down on their heads. Also, they stank. It occurred to me then that I had to look and smell as awful as my companions, and I became momentarily depressed.

"We smell bad," I said.

Yipes and John looked at each other. Then each raised an arm and sniffed in the general direction of the exposed area. Unsatisfied, they stepped closer to me, sniffed at the air once again, and turned away.

"I'm afraid it's you, my dear," said Yipes. "You're as ripe as a July tomato."

John nodded his approval.

"Really?" I said, and I began sniffing the air around me.

Murphy, who was always my advocate in such matters, immediately darted up Yipes's leg, grabbed hold of his vest with all four claws, and dug his little head into

Yipes's armpit. Yipes squirmed about, spinning this way and that, until at last Murphy came up for air, a look of disgust on his little face.

"This one smells *terrible*," cried Murphy. "And *that* one." He looked over at John, whose arms were folded firmly across his chest. "That one there is three times the size of Yipes and sweats by the bucketful."

At least I wasn't the only one in need of a bath. This was a small if meaningless comfort.

We were all looking at the map when John spun around and looked up to the right on the barren hill in front of us.

"I feel it again," he said. "Someone or something is near."

He pointed across the ravine at a clump of half-dead bushes next to a small rise of dirt. "Let's huddle down beneath the brush and stay out of sight until we figure out what to do. I fear the Valley of Thorns may be just over that hill."

We hurried to where the bushes were and crouched together in the dirt. The cover it provided was not sufficient to hide us entirely, but at least we were out of the wide-open space of the ravine. The day had crept into early afternoon and the sun was hot, but not so much as it had been thus far on our journey. There was a faint breeze, and though it was not altogether cool, it had a freshness unlike the baking heat of past days, as if this wind had its origin in a colder place.

"If it's true that we find ourselves at the base of the Valley of Thorns, do we have any idea what to do now?" asked Odessa, the ears upon her mighty gray head sticking straight up and alert.

"Where's Murphy?" I asked, not finding him among us in the thicket. We were all looking back and forth when the sound of pebbles sliding down the hill came from above us. At first I was terrified of what I might see, but when I looked up, I saw that Murphy had darted away and was scampering up the hill, his tiny legs sending him on a zigzag course as he hid beneath tufts of weeds. He was quickly halfway up, where he looked back, jumped, and waved his limbs all around. Then he turned and raced off again.

"I don't know what to do with him," said Yipes, shaking his head slowly. "He hasn't a shred of common sense."

"Maybe the smell of your armpit scrambled his brains," I said.

"Quiet, you two," said John. "I've lost him in the brush near the top."

I removed my spyglass, the same one I'd taken from my mother and used in Bridewell the summer before. The lens that Pervis had broken out had been replaced, and it seemed as good as new when my mother offered it to me as a gift on my thirteenth birthday. I slid it open with a snap and handed it to John. The spyglass had been of some use along the way already, but this was the first time I was truly relieved to have brought it with me.

We were all quiet for a moment while John tried to find Murphy on the hill.

"There, I have him. He's just reaching the top now."

I waited in silence, watching as Yipes secretly raised his right arm and smelled the air beneath it, and then I could hold my tongue no longer in my worry over Murphy.

"What's happening? Can you still see him?" Just then we all heard a shriek from above and looked into the sky. Squire was circling the air, watching as the scene unfolded. I wished then that I, too, could fly, if only for a moment, so that I could see everything that lay before us on the other side of the hill.

"You know, this really makes very good sense, now that I've had a moment to consider it," said Yipes.

"What's happening?" I asked, ignoring Yipes in my worry over the plight of our friend.

"No, really," Yipes continued. "I don't think he's gone mad, at least not completely. When you think it through, who or whatever lies beyond the hill might well be watching for intruders. A squirrel poses no threat. In fact, he probably goes entirely unnoticed. I only wish he would have let us come to that conclusion together before dashing off on his own."

John closed the spyglass and held it out to me without looking in my direction.

"He's halfway back down. There," he said, pointing to a small brown clump flitting this way and that down the hill.

Murphy rejoined us, completely out of breath and momentarily unable to speak. We gathered close around him until finally he was able to tell us what he had seen in a single well-chosen word.

"Giants," he said. He took a few more labored breaths, looked around at the group, and added a bit more.

"Lots of them."

# CHAPTER 12

# THE VALLEY OF
# THORNS

We all sat silent and still as Murphy told us what he'd seen from the top of the hill, a long pause every now and then as I shared this information with Yipes. Though Yipes seemed perfectly happy to hear the details second-hand, I felt bad for him only hearing a long trail of squeaks as Murphy spoke.

There was a steep drop-off on the other side, followed by a hundred yards of valley with terrain much like the Dark Hills. After this came a large swath of what appeared to be thin tree stumps sticking up out of the earth from side to side as far as Murphy could see. Beneath the stumps was a gathering of brown stubble, and walking upon the stubble were ten or so men of remarkable size, who Murphy took to be giants. In his further description, it appeared to Murphy that the trees had not been cut where they stood, for they were too closely placed together and arranged in a perfect pattern. The trees or wooden poles — Murphy was less sure of their nature the longer he spoke — stuck out of the ground at varying heights, some so low to the ground that one would measure them in inches, others several feet high, and still more that were five feet and above. In all cases, the stumps or poles were black at the base and carved to a sharp point at the top, where the tips were the color of blood.

The stumps continued along the valley floor for something on the order of a hundred yards more, and past these the valley became alive with abundant shades of green. Not far beyond the green was the striking presence of a bright blue lake. Murphy called it "magnificent in its size and color."

"Castalia," said Odessa. The word hung in the air until it was pushed away by a question from John.

"Are the giants too far from the edge of the hill to be reached with a well-placed arrow?"

Murphy looked thoughtfully back up at the hill, trying to remember how far off they had really been.

"You might be able to hit the edge, but the giants walked among the poles toward the middle. Plus I thought I saw a head appear from the earth, so they might have dug trenches, too. Either that or there are some very short giants down there scattered among the big ones. I think a sky filled with arrows, shot down from the top of the hill, would only fall wasted in the valley."

John and Yipes were the only ones with bows and a small reserve of arrows, so it didn't seem likely that we'd be able to fend off even a single giant.

"One thing is for sure: We have to find a place to

hide," said Odessa. "They must be in the habit of sending scouts to the very ground we stand on."

We looked as far as we could in every direction and found with unfortunate clarity that the only shelter to be had was back in the direction from which we had come. We'd be seen by anyone patrolling the top of the hill.

"There are at least three good sets of large rocks a half mile back," said Yipes. "We could stay here until night and move back to one of them, or take our chances in broad daylight."

Neither option sounded very appealing to me. Where we sat, we only had a few miserable bushes to hide behind. And yet venturing out into the wide open of the Dark Hills in the middle of the day seemed foolhardy with giants milling around so close by.

"Can you hail Squire?" John asked Yipes.

"I believe I can," said Yipes. "But to what purpose?"

"I have an idea she might be useful."

Yipes stood up and pulled a red cotton handkerchief from his vest pocket. He held it over his head and waved it to and fro for some time, careful to stay behind a bush so he could only be seen from the sky. Squire ignored him entirely and continued circling high in the air above us.

"You've trained that one well," said Odessa. "Can you make her roll over and play dead?"

Yipes waved the red handkerchief more furiously until at last he agreed that Squire was indeed ignoring him. He looked around nervously until he caught sight of

Murphy, who was absently working on a walnut I'd given him upon his return.

"There is one way that almost always works," said Yipes, and then he knelt down next to Murphy and looked at us as if he were about to do something underhanded.

"How is the nut?" he asked.

"Fine, thank you," said Murphy, though Yipes only heard him squeaking.

"I'm so glad you're enjoying it."

Just then Yipes tapped Murphy upon the head, ran his hand along his back, and grabbed hold of his tail.

There is one thing a squirrel cannot stand, and Yipes had just perpetrated it on our little friend. Instinct will send a squirrel caught by the tail into a fit of biting, scratching, and screaming, and Yipes was well aware of this. He quickly moved out into the open, away from the bushes, and began swinging Murphy in circles over his head, which kept the sharp teeth from whipping around and finding his forearm. All the while Murphy was screaming his head off, and though this was not the loudest sound one might hear, a hawk has exceptional hearing (not to mention outstanding sight), and Squire dived into the ravine looking for a trapped squirrel almost immediately.

As soon as Squire started for us, Yipes stopped spinning Murphy, crouched near the ground, and let go of his tail. Murphy rolled several times and landed punch-drunk on his feet in the wide open. He wobbled back and forth and then fell on his side, the twirling having dizzied his mind.

"Grab him!" yelled Yipes. Squire was within a hundred feet of us and heading straight for Murphy. I was the closest, so I bolted the two steps I needed to and crouched down over Murphy, covering him with my back. Squire pulled up short and circled low, then landed on Yipes's outstretched arm.

"That went rather well, don't you think?" said Yipes.

Murphy recovered, and I cradled him with one arm while I handed him back his nut. He grabbed hold of it and began working at the shell again.

John approached the hawk and put a hand near his head. Squire remained calm as John slowly moved the hand closer and finally touched her with two fingers on the neck. None of us, John included, could know what Squire was thinking or if she really understood the things we said. Still, John spoke to the stately creature in a quiet voice.

"Can you tell us if they are coming?" He ran his two fingers along the neck to the top of the wing, picked up the fingers, and started again at the neck, then softly spoke to the bird one more time.

"Will you warn us if they move for the hill?" He took his hand away, reached into his pocket, and presented a bit of dried meat to Squire.

"Let her go," he said. Yipes threw his arm up, and

Squire's powerful wings moved her off toward the distant sky. We watched until she resumed her circular motion over the hill, quietly floating above the earth, watching all that lay beneath her on the ground.

"We could also leave Murphy to watch," Odessa said. "I'm a prize they are likely to come after with arrows, but Murphy they would ignore."

"He wouldn't make it through the day," said Yipes. "It's amazing he's not dead already."

At first I was puzzled by his reply, and then all at once I understood.

"Squire," I said.

"Indeed," said Yipes. "She's a lovely bird, but a rodent is a rodent and nature is nature." He looked up into the sky. "That bird will devour Murphy if we leave him all alone at the top of the hill. Look at him, he can't sit still, and in this case his life would depend on it. We can't risk it."

I could feel Murphy trying to wriggle free from me, to escape and run back up the hill. As Yipes had observed, he had no fear, so I kept him close and calmed him down until he agreed that he should stay with us.

"We must run with all our might back to the rocks, the largest of the three groupings to the right, and we must do it now and trust Squire to warn us if the giants emerge," said John.

It was quickly agreed, and after a brief glance up to see that Squire was still circling, we began running back into the Dark Hills. Odessa was by far the fastest among us, and she raced out ahead. The rest of us stayed clumped together and tried not to trample the brush too much for fear that a scout might see where we'd been and become alerted to our presence.

I listened for Squire over labored breathing and the noise of packs bouncing upon backs and feet scuffling over dried earth. We were a few minutes into our run, all of us tiring badly, when Odessa reached the rocks in front of us. The rest of us still had a hundred yards to go, and though most of the work was behind us, that last stretch seemed like miles and miles in my exhaustion.

With fifty yards left to go it seemed as though I could almost touch the rocks with an outstretched hand. The group of us caught our second wind. This was further helped along by Squire, who began screeching from the expanse behind us, a sound that scared me into a full sprint until I fell to my knees breathless behind the rocks.

No one spoke while we recovered from the run, which made Squire's screeching all the more terrifying. I hoped, as did the rest, that she'd only been happy to see us reach our destination or that she'd caught sight of another hawk and they were alerting each other of their presence.

The rocks were not as protective as we'd hoped, and we had to sit or lie down to avoid being seen from the top of the hill. The situation was further complicated by the discovery that two of the rocks sat together and one was several feet to the left and all alone in the dirt. Each of the stones was large enough to hide a body or two, but not much more. Odessa had arrived in front of the lone rock, and there she stayed. The rest of us were crumpled together behind the two remaining rocks, which were barely big enough to conceal us. Murphy darted across the three feet that lay between us and jumped onto Odessa's back.

"She's stopped her shrieking," I whispered, and then I realized how unnecessary whispering was since we'd gone so far out into the Dark Hills. I continued in a normal tone of voice. "Murphy, jump up on the rock and tell us what you see."

This he did, nervously flitting from side to side on the fat stone.

"Stop moving around so much," said Yipes. "You'll only draw their attention."

"I don't see anything moving on the hill. It's perfectly still," said Murphy, and then he jumped back down onto Odessa's back.

Yipes, John, and I rose slowly until the tops of our heads peeked out over the rocks and the hill came into view. It was true — no one was on the hilltop. We all breathed a sigh of relief.

We became momentarily relaxed and raised our heads a bit more over the edge of the rocks. Then Squire landed directly in front of us, her powerful wings flapping her to a stop. The three of us were so startled we fell back from the rocks and landed on our elbows.

"Maybe you could give a little warning before you arrive next time," said Yipes, beginning to stand so he might be able to wipe himself off.

"Wait," I said. Then I turned to Murphy and asked him to jump on the rock and look once again. Squire flew off, her wings so powerful they stirred the dust beneath the rocks, and we waited on our backs.

"Don't move," said Murphy. "Three giants, all with spyglasses aimed this way, are standing on the hilltop." Sweat dripped down my temple and I quietly relayed this information to the others. I stayed completely still and out of sight along with the rest.

Murphy jumped down off the rock and ran off somewhere I could not see. The seconds turned to minutes.

"I'm scared," I said aloud. I felt like I might begin to cry, the weight of our circumstances quickly becoming more than I could handle. I took a few strands of my hair into my mouth and chewed them, a nervous habit I hadn't fallen into for a long time. John took hold of my hand and rubbed the backs of my fingers. His thumb was incredibly worn and rough. It had a protective, powerful way about it, as if it had been through much worse and survived.

"They've gone." It was Murphy, who had returned to the rock. "The hilltop is empty and Squire is circling again."

"It would seem that our winged companion has become quite useful," said John. I brushed the strands of

81

hair out of my mouth and let go of his hand so I could sit up without trouble. Then we all gathered behind the two rocks and quietly prepared the small bit of food and water that remained.

We sat hidden behind the rocks until the sun set behind the hill. Not long after that, everything was quiet and dark. It was nighttime in the Dark Hills, and we were without food, water, or shelter.

## CHAPTER 13

# AN UNEXPECTED DEVELOPMENT

The lights were moving swiftly down the face of the hill, but they did not bob and jump as they might if men were running with torches. They were giants, and they were simply walking toward us. It frightened me to think how quickly they could overtake us on foot if they chose to. Odessa began a deep, low growl as we watched the torches continue their descent.

"Try to stay calm, Odessa. You'll give us away," whispered Yipes. He and John had both set arrows into their bows to try to protect us. We had come with little weaponry; a few small knives and two bows were the whole of our defense.

A hurried conversation ensued. Should we stay hidden behind the rocks? Should we run into the Dark Hills where no protection could be found, hoping they turned and went back? All the while, the lights kept coming, slowly closing the gap between us.

"I feel it again, the same presence I've felt all day," said John.

"Of course you do," said Yipes. "The giants are right there in front of us."

While they spoke I realized that Murphy had disappeared once again. Could he have darted out ahead to bite the legs of those awful creatures? The giants were off the hill and walking in the open expanse between us now, Murphy was missing, and we had nowhere to hide. I whispered Murphy's name and when he didn't answer I began to panic. Odessa uttered a low, barely audible growl. We all looked hopelessly at one another, and a distinct feeling of despair hung in the air.

"Quiet," said John.

Odessa stopped growling, and there was no noise but for our breathing. Then I heard the scamper of tiny feet, and all at once Murphy was among us again, shouting incoherently in his squeaky voice, excited beyond words and unable to contain himself.

"Calm down," whispered Yipes. "Can't you see the giants are coming toward us?"

Murphy tried desperately to calm himself until finally he was able to form a few simple words.

"Don't be afraid," he said. "Just stay quiet."

This was a strange thing to say, especially given that Murphy himself was so agitated he could hardly calm himself long enough to put together a plain sentence. Our confusion was further heightened when he darted out into the Dark Hills, away from the advancing giants. We lost sight of him again.

"He's finally gone completely out of his mind," said Yipes, his head shaking back and forth. "I suppose it was only a matter of time." Then he went back to preparing his bow and watching the torches in the distance.

Odessa turned and growled in the direction Murphy had gone, after which Murphy came darting out of the blackness again, his small frame like a formless shadow rushing along the ground.

I had a sensation then that wasn't quite feeling or hearing but a mix of both at the same time. I looked into the night and pressed against the rocks, the feeling growing more scary and real as the seconds passed. And then I saw him coming out of the darkness — an immense, formless mass. Out of the night came a giant, and before we could think to run, he towered over us not unlike the walls of Bridewell had in years past. He was gigantic, beyond comprehension in his magnificent size. A sword was sheathed in his belt.

"The arrows will do you no good," said the giant. "You should put them away." His voice was surprisingly soothing and aged; this was not a young giant but an old one. His face was difficult to see in the darkness.

"Armon?" questioned John. "Could it be?"

"The very one," replied the giant. "Come to save you in your hour of need, just as Warvold instructed."

There was very little light, but the moon was on the rise and the stars were thickening by the minute. I began to distinguish his face. It was just as I'd hoped it would be: very wise and very kind; old, but not ancient; strong in a graceful way.

"Gather your things and move as quietly as you can," he told us. "They place the rocks here on purpose. As you see they are the only places to hide, and it is here as always that they will come looking for intruders."

Armon reached down and picked up our empty wineskins, which seemed extraordinarily small slung over his shoulder. On the other shoulder hung a large leather pack, three feet wide and five or more feet in length. I wondered what might be inside.

Yipes walked up to Armon and stood in amazement at his feet. He looked at John and said, "Now you know how I feel." Then he reached out and touched the giant's knee.

"Move away from the rocks, if you would," said the giant. We all obeyed without hesitation.

He proceeded to pick up each of the gigantic stones one by one, the largest of them almost as big as my desk back home, and moved them four giant steps closer to the hill. This he did with great care and speed, placing the stones in the same formation they had been in, dusting his tracks after each trip out. Not the least bit out of breath from the effort, he stood before us and pointed into the Dark Hills, away from the oncoming lights.

"Run, but go quietly as you do," he said.

Armon walked slowly behind us, covering tracks as best he could as we went. A short while later he told us to stop, kneel down, and remain silent.

"They have arrived at the rocks," he whispered. The

torches had split into three, one at each of the formations we had seen earlier in the day. We paid careful attention to the rocks we had hidden behind as the light danced along the ground, rose into the air, and started moving back toward the hill. We watched as the three torches came together once again and moved away from us into the night.

Armon knelt before me, his wonderful face close enough now to see clearly, wrinkled with the years and yet somehow ageless. His skin had no beard or stubble like a man's — it was clean and perfect. Waves of black hair ran over his ears and onto his shoulders.

"You must be Alexa," he said. He placed his fingers on the side of my face, each as thick as five of my own and more than twice as long. I was overcome with emotion; his presence among us was like we were in a real fairy tale, bringing hope to a hopeless situation. Could it be that Elyon was among us? If so, Armon was the greatest gift he could have given. With Armon's touch my fear melted away. The mighty giant had arrived to protect us. He was the one giant among them all who was bound to Elyon and so bound to us.

He rose again to his feet without another word and looked up at the stars in search of direction.

"I have prepared a place where we can rest," Armon said. "It's not far from here."

"What's it like up there?" asked Yipes, standing again at the foot of the giant. He seemed terribly curious about

Armon, as though the opposing nature of their size gave them something in common. Armon put one hand around Yipes's middle and lifted him ten feet off the ground into the night sky, where he looked him straight in the eye.

"I have heard about you," said Armon.

"Somehow that doesn't surprise me," Yipes replied, his short legs dangling helplessly over the ground.

Armon set Yipes down and began walking parallel to the great hill. Murphy leaped onto the giant's leg, ran the length of his body, and sat on his shoulder. Armon paid Murphy no attention other than to gently tap him twice on the head with his big finger.

"The last of the stones," he said, as if reading from an ancient text. "I had another stone long ago, but its powers have been erased by time. I hear only squeaking when the squirrel opens his mouth, but I gather you hear much more."

He looked at me then and, though it was dark, I could tell he was smiling.

Armon slowed and put his hand on John, covering his back entirely with the palm, his fingers wrapping around John's arm on the other side.

"Warvold spoke highly of you," said Armon, still looking forward as he walked. "You and Yipes and Alexa. There were times the three of you were all he talked about for days on end." And then Armon looked down at

John. "He was of the opinion that behind your weathered face lies untold wisdom."

John put his hand on Armon's great forearm and squeezed what little of it he could get his fingers around.

"I'm delighted to have you among us," said John. "With Warvold's story unfolding these past days, I've hoped for some help. This is beyond my wildest dreams."

While they spoke, a thousand questions ran through my head. I was beginning to have some trouble keeping them to myself.

"What became of Catherine and Laura?" I asked.

Armon looked at Yipes and found that he was having some difficulty keeping up with the rest of us. We were all walking faster than normal, and even though Yipes was energetic, the fact remained that his legs were tiny compared to Armon's. Armon removed his hand from John's back, picked up Yipes, and placed him on his shoulder, which put Yipes's head at something on the order of twelve feet in the air.

"You're too kind," said Yipes, while Murphy scampered even higher than he had been and sat on Yipes's shoulder. Murphy on Yipes on Armon — it was beginning to look like a circus act from where I stood below, and it further illuminated the unique nature of our group. I was beginning to see fewer of our weaknesses and more of our strengths; the events of the day were a reminder of how each of us had certain abilities that the rest did not.

It was as if we were each a part of a whole body — one the hands, another the legs, and so on — dependent on one another and working best when we performed in unity. I felt inadequate then, unsure what part of this body I might be.

"We have only another hour to walk, and then we shall rest and talk of how to overcome the Valley of Thorns," said Armon. "I must warn you that we will only have a short while to sleep, a few hours at the most. We must rise before dawn and set our plan into motion."

He looked at my pleading face and saw how much I wanted to hear about Catherine and Laura.

"There will be plenty of time to address our plans after I tell you what became of the girls," he said.

And then he spoke of what Warvold had left untold, a steady breeze in our faces as we went.

CHAPTER 14

# WHAT REMAINS OF THE STORY IS TOLD

Everything changed for me in the passing of that hour. Armon spoke with an incredible authority, in such a way that all the story's pieces fell delicately into place. As we walked I knew nothing of the fearful things that awaited us — Victor Grindall and his line of sons, the torches I'd seen on the hill, the wild dogs of Castalia's dumping grounds. For that hour Armon's commanding presence was all my world could hold.

"Not long after Catherine and Laura arrived in the clock tower, it became clear that the three of us would need to leave the region," he began. "We needed to travel far away, to a place where we could not be found. We had to take the stones with us and protect them from Grindall and the evil forces that guided him.

"Already Grindall was sending out his men and his giants to search for me and the stones. Soon enough their searching would lead them into the City of Dogs, and our hiding place would be found."

Murphy scurried down from his perch on Yipes's shoulder and landed on the ground. He took two quick strides and leaped into my arms where I held him against my chest, glad to have him near me.

"Two days after arriving at the clock tower, at the darkest point of moonlessness, we ventured into the night. We encountered one of the packs of wild dogs, twenty or more in number, and I placed the girls high on my back, out of danger."

Armon set his hand on the butt of his sword, a weapon more than six feet in length, the end dangling at his ankles in its sheath.

"My sword was of much use on that night," he said. "The first pack of dogs relented, but others crept in as we traveled the length of the old city and its piles of debris. On that night we counted over a hundred dogs, some in packs as large as thirty, others in groups as small as five, all of them ravaged with disease and rage. A single bite from one of these sickly creatures would surely bring illness, madness, and eventually even death.

"At the edge of the City of Dogs is a large forest that runs for several miles along the western shore of the lake. As we made our escape, the forest was crawling with giants and men in search of me and the stones. But Grindall made a grievous error, for at that time giants were in service to both Grindall and those of their own race. There in the forest, two men saw us. These two called a warning with a horn, and help arrived in the form of three giants. The giants took hold of the men and threw them against a tree, dashing out their brains in the process."

"This story keeps getting better and better," said Yipes, a grin hiding his lips beneath his mustache as he looked down at me on the ground.

"I spoke to the three giants," continued Armon. "And it was agreed that they would set us free of Castalia to roam the wide reaches of The Land of Elyon in search of a new home, and that we would keep the remaining stones with us and protect them. We were taken to the Valley of Thorns, a place where only giants roam, and we were each of us seen by yet more giants who agreed to set us free. Over the great hill into the Dark Hills we ventured, with no idea where the journey might end.

"We had no food or water and precious little time to escape. So I took the girls once again on my back and ran through the night into the Dark Hills. In the morning I slept an hour and then continued in the same way until night fell once more. In two days' time we stood at the base of Mount Norwood, a place we would call home for many years thereafter."

"You lived on the mountain near Lathbury?" I asked, astounded at how close he'd been.

"The very one," Armon answered. It struck me then how I might have walked right past places Armon had been while I was on my first journey with Yipes outside the walls of Bridewell.

"We traveled high into the lush green of the mountain and made for ourselves a home there where we watched and waited. On very clear days, far across the Dark Hills, we could see the outline of the other great mountain that stands upright to the east of Castalia."

It was Mount Laythen that Armon spoke of, a mountain much taller and wider than Mount Norwood, not so different in size than Armon was to Yipes. Mount Laythen was the highest peak in The Land of Elyon, with a fat round bottom fifty miles wide.

"Catherine developed a deep fascination with all of the stones that remained," said Armon. "Especially the one that she took herself. She was completely obsessed with protecting it and understanding what she could of the rest. Soon she took advantage of their power and befriended all sorts of wild animals, one of which was an exquisite mountain lion. In the past Catherine had been unwilling to show the remaining stones to her animal friends, but something about the lion was different, and so she took him to where the stones were hidden. Together they examined the remaining twenty stones, and the lion was able to see something Catherine could not. Some of the stones were different, inscribed with an ancient language. With the help of the lion, Catherine separated the stones and found that only six were marked in this special way. The fourteen that were not marked were taken to a small pond near the base of the mountain and left at the edge for those who might find them, while the other six were taken to a secret pool high atop Mount Norwood, mixed among ordinary stones, and left to be found by those who might stumble onto them as Elyon had ordained.

"Catherine and the mountain lion spent much time together, and the lion told Catherine all that he had seen in the stones, what the ancient language looked like, and how he was able to understand what was written. From this knowledge, Catherine made a habit of finding objects and carving patterns on them with secret hidden messages and pictures. In time she would learn to do such things with intricate tools on smaller and smaller items, until finally, much later, Catherine was able to do these etchings on items as small as a stone that might be carried around the neck of an ordinary library cat. She liked to call them Jocastas."

"It can't be so," I said.

"Catherine was Renny Warvold," said John, not as if he'd known all along but as though he'd figured it out just then, as I had.

Armon looked at us both with kindness and nodded slowly, a strange, sad hope in his eyes.

"Some time after she etched Elyon's words on each of the six stones, it came to pass that a young adventurer, many years of wandering behind him, came to rest on Mount Norwood. He had explored the land to the farthest cliffs, beyond Ainsworth to the northern side, and to the heights of Mount Laythen where he looked down on the plight of Castalia. He had traveled through the Dark Hills, the magnificent forests, and even into the haunting lair of the Sly Field. He had visited each of the two cities along the northern cliffs and the one to the west. In all his travels he never found a place more peaceful and joyous than Mount Norwood, and it was here that he returned after Catherine, Laura, and I had already been living there for a dozen years."

"Thomas Warvold," I whispered, the pieces of the puzzle coming together now.

"As Elyon would have it, the young Warvold stumbled onto the pool of Jocastas, quite sure that he had found the greatest treasure in The Land of Elyon. The girls were now grown women, and together with them I met Warvold for the first time at the edge of the pool. Warvold had seen giants before, but I was very different from all the others. Having had quite a lot of experience with seeing all manner of oddities, he was not so startled as you might suppose. Very quickly the four of us became acquainted. We went about the ritual of presenting Warvold with a Jocasta, and spent a time enjoying one another's company in the surrounding beauty of Mount Norwood.

"As you might have guessed, Catherine and Warvold fell in love, and soon thereafter the two of them began to tire of living alone in the mountains. It was decided that Warvold would go to Ainsworth and find those among the city that he might recruit into building a new kingdom past the Great Ravine, a city surrounded entirely by walls, which would afford protection from the dangers of the wild. It was further decided that before accompanying him, Catherine would change her name to Renny, in the event that anyone within the settled world knew of her and the legend of Armon."

I was at once astounded by all that Renny had been through. I tried desperately to remember her, but I had been only a small child when she passed away, and I could dig up no images to remind me of her. I only knew that I missed her more than I thought I should. I wished she were still alive.

"In the years that followed, Lunenburg came into being, Nicolas was born to Renny and Thomas, and the kingdom of Bridewell surfaced in The Land of Elyon."

Armon stopped then and knelt down so I could see his expression clearly.

"Shortly after the walls were completed, I began to feel a terrible dark presence from the distant land of Castalia. So I traveled there — or here, I should say — to where we now find ourselves. In the dead of night I crept to the top of the hill. What I saw there I must now, unfortunately, share with you."

He motioned everyone closer, and we stood before the kneeling giant.

"From the very beginning there have been stories among the giants — sacred stories, many of which have become more fable than truth as the human side of us dominates more and more. Our former home — the Tenth City — has been forgotten in the passing of time."

Armon paused, digging up the past in his head. He seemed to be weighing what he should and shouldn't say.

"Humans are a forgetful and doubtful race of beings," he continued. "To remember things of a distant past is something of a difficulty for them, and so it is with my own kind in the tenth reign of Grindall, our memories of the Tenth City washing away."

Armon stopped again and looked at the great hill, searching for signs of life in the moonlight. Then he turned back to us and went on, his face downcast.

"Do you know about the bats?" he asked.

He was surprised to find that we knew of them and had even encountered them in the Dark Hills. He seemed concerned about this.

"Where did you see them? Was it near?" he asked.

"No, it wasn't near," said Yipes with a soothing tone. "It was many miles back, closer to Bridewell than here."

Armon seemed to listen very carefully, still agitated.

"I can never be seen by them," he said, and then he told us why.

"There is a swarm of a thousand bats, sent by Abaddon from where he dwells, and these bats have but one purpose — to peck and tear at the heads of the giants, to infect them with Abaddon's will.

"Imagine a giant the same size as me with its skull emptied of hair but for clumps and strands growing sickly around the rim and over the ears. Imagine the head and face marked with scabs and open sores that never run dry, the teeth rotted out and missing or blackened — a hideous, disfigured creature answering to Abaddon's will."

Armon stood up then and towered over us.

"That's what happens to giants who are found by the swarm of bats."

He closed his eyes, letting the words sink in. I got the feeling things were about to get even scarier.

"I am the last of what remains of my race. The rest have already been found by the swarm," he said, opening his eyes. "What lies beyond the great hill is not more of my kind, but the darkest evil in The Land of Elyon — ninety-eight gargantuan monsters with but one goal before them: to destroy us so Elyon can never return."

"The swarm has narrowed its hunt to only one?" John asked, his worrisome question hanging in the air like thick black tar until Armon gazed into the Dark Hills and spoke once more.

"They move in the night, forever searching until they discover me and infect me like the rest." He looked at us then with a glimmer of hope. "We must win the battle before they find me."

He started walking again into the darkness, and I found myself running to be near him and find comfort in his presence. I was happy when Armon started talking again, his peaceful voice pushing my visions of dreadful beasts away.

"There is some good news among all the bad," he began again. "I have not quite finished with the story. The infected giants are no more powerful than they were before, and although forceful, they can be defeated if one knows how. Further, and of far more importance, to kill all the giants would be to destroy Abaddon's vast army and leave him exposed, furious, and reckless."

"But ninety-eight of them?" I said.

"It is a bit daunting," said Armon. "But you must never forget that Elyon, in his own mysterious way, a way which we cannot understand, is on our side. The creator of both human and Seraph has chosen us, and I can only hope that in his vast wisdom he will show us how we might prevail against all odds."

We had been walking for a while. Armon looked around in all directions.

"This will do," he said. "I've brought some food and water. Set out your things and eat if you like. You will have only a short while to sleep."

We were still out in the open and the great hill lay before us.

"Isn't this more exposed than we'd like?" asked Odessa, which I in turn translated to Armon.

"There's no other place to be had, I'm afraid. I'll watch through the night, but I don't expect to see anyone near here."

I set my small pack on the crusty dirt and took a

handful of nuts and berries out from the stash Armon provided.

"If you're not too tired I'd like to tell you the last of the story. I believe it may help to properly motivate you in the coming days."

Armon sat down among us and gathered his thoughts to speak a final time about the things of the past. While he considered what to say, I watched the night sky with its countless stars and its moon, and I wondered about the universe and all that had been created, why the stars and the moon rose at night and the sun in the day, how vast it must be, how I could never understand the infinite measure of its size.

Odessa rarely chose me when it came time to rest, but on this night she did, and she lay down along my side with her head next to mine. Murphy hopped onto her back and made a bed of her soft gray hair, and the three of us were comforted by one another.

"The tenth reign of Grindall came into existence not long after I departed Castalia," Armon began. "I know this prince of darkness, this tenth Victor Grindall. His reign began through trickery and murder, and immediately he focused everything on finding the remaining stones.

"But in all his efforts Victor Grindall failed to recover the missing treasure. This greatly displeased Abaddon. So it came to pass that Grindall sent the giants beyond the Dark Hills to find the stones, to places they'd never searched before.

"Before long the giants were within reach of the wall at Bridewell. Pervis Kotcher, the head of the guards, was the first to see them from his tower at the Lunenburg gate. This was a moment he understood might come, for Thomas and Renny had told him if giants were ever seen in the Dark Hills, he should hide the fact and send all the guards off the towers. If other guards had seen, Pervis was to collect them and bring them before Warvold, and the rest of the kingdom was to remain unaware of the horrible danger beyond the wall.

"Renny was the first person Pervis found as he searched the lodge for either of the Warvolds, and he told her of the giants approaching in the distance. Renny instructed Pervis to find Thomas. Then, without delay, she ran to the library and entered the secret tunnel that leads under the city and into the mountains."

Armon leaned back on his mighty hands while the rest of us sat wide-eyed before him.

"Once in the tunnel, there is a hidden door that, when opened, leads the short distance out into the Dark Hills. This door Renny opened, and not long after that the giants arrived at the wall. She stood alone and unprotected among them."

"Why, Armon? Why would she do such a thing?" I asked.

"She thought, quite rightly, that if she could offer herself it might appease the giants. Capturing the one who had taken the stones might be a good enough reason to return to the Dark Tower. It would certainly be a noteworthy find. And so Renny offered to go with them, insisting that she would only tell what she knew to Victor Grindall himself.

"About this time, Warvold and Pervis arrived at the Lunenburg tower. The giants, who Warvold would later say were already possessed by Abaddon, were big enough to break through the wall if they wanted to. But they only wanted the remaining stones, and this they demanded of Warvold. They would have the remaining stones or the whole of Bridewell would be overrun and everything within the kingdom would be destroyed.

"Weaponry was not advanced in Bridewell, and the city relied almost entirely on archers for defense. The giants carried two things that worried Warvold greatly — large metal shields and bags filled with stones the size of watermelons, which he rightly guessed they could throw with great accuracy. The hideous giant heads dripping with sweat and open sores, the shields combined with great black armor — these things conspired against Warvold and the armament he possessed. These were huge creatures, well armed and adequately protected. A hundred of them would wipe out everyone in Bridewell and move on to Turlock and Lathbury when they were through."

Armon looked at Yipes, who was sitting upright, eyes almost comically wide, completely enthralled by the story. Like so many of us from Bridewell Common, our little friend simply loved to hear a good tale. I'm not sure he fully grasped that the story included us, the dangers looming larger every time Armon opened his mouth.

"Thomas saw the moment for what it was," continued Armon. "A pivotal encounter in the fight over which forces would control The Land of Elyon, forces of evil or good. But the price was higher than he had imagined it could be. His own life he would have gladly given, but he had great difficulty sacrificing those of his people or his beloved wife. He knew where the six stones lay hidden in the secret pool on Mount Norwood. He could lead these awful creatures there and they would disappear once again into the Dark Hills. But what evil would overcome the land if he allowed this to happen, and how quickly would an even darker force return and bound over the walls if he gave away the secret?

"Warvold would not reveal what he knew, and on that terrible day Catherine was taken from him. It was said that if she could not produce the whereabouts of the stones, she would be locked away in the deepest part of the Dark Tower at Castalia, until the remaining stones were found and returned to pay her ransom.

"I don't know what Catherine told them or how she has kept the giants away from Bridewell these ten years.

Maybe she has sent them searching in the City of Dogs or in the streams of Mount Laythen. But one thing I feel is certain: She remains among us. Catherine, the woman you know as Renny, is alive, locked in the dungeon in the tower across the lake."

# PART 2

# CHAPTER 15

# FIRE AND RAIN

"Wake up, Alexa. The fire is already started." It was dark and cold as I shivered awake, my body aching from yet another night of broken sleep against the floor of the Dark Hills. Everyone else was already stirring or standing, looking across the valley where an orange glow rippled along the top of the hills. This was not the sight of the sun rising over the earth; it was something closer and more dangerous.

"What's happening?" I asked, rubbing sleep out of my eyes as I rose, feeling the toughness of the ground beneath my tender feet. I bent low to itch the scabs on my shins from which I continued to find no relief. It was still night or very early morning, and everything was dark but the fire on the hill and the stars overhead.

"Armon has been busy while we've slept," said Yipes through a yawn and a stretch. I walked to where they stood and gazed at the hill.

"The wind rolls down the mountain and into the valley," said Armon. "And thunderclouds often gather along the rim of the great mountain. Vast brushfires along the hill are not so uncommon during this time of summer. Everything turns black, only to be reborn again in the spring with new underbrush. The cycle continues year after year. Some years there are many fires and some years there are few, but often humans or nature ignites the dead brush."

My eyes had adjusted to the starry light and the distant glow of fire on the hill. Armon knelt next to me, pointing into the darkness.

"I started the fire there with my flint, at the base of Mount Laythen, and the wind carried it along the hill and over to the other side." Already the fire had spread over the top of the hill and along its front to the valley where we stood. I could only assume it had spread to the other side of the hill as well.

"There are thousands of poles that make up the Valley of Thorns. They are covered in thick tar at the base, and the brush beneath them will burn through as it always does. The giants will pull back from the Valley of Thorns and stand at its edge, protecting the forest in case the flames come too close, until the fire passes through. Then they will walk through and stamp out any glowing embers that remain. By morning our opportunity will have passed."

The orange glow of the fire line was mesmerizing in the darkness, like a twisted snake upon the land, writhing and devouring everything in its path. It glowed hot and wide when the wind gusted through, and sat low and patient when the billows ceased.

"Gather your things and breathe deeply while there is

fresh air. The smoke that provides our cover will make the going difficult," Armon warned.

"How far away is the great mountain?" asked John, trying to get his bearings and understand where we would enter the city.

"From here, probably twenty miles," Armon answered.

"You couldn't have traveled that far while we slept, Armon. Forty miles in only a few hours is hard to imagine, even for you," said Yipes.

"Two hours and twelve minutes, to be exact," said Armon. "And you thought I'd only been eating blackberries and lounging about in the mountains all these years, getting fat and happy."

"Yes, but *forty miles?*" Yipes objected. Armon had nothing more to say on the subject, and the night air stood silent, a cool breeze driving the flames closer still.

We walked away from the flames, in line with the hill. The fire had not yet drawn close, but it was traveling fast, and it seemed to me that within an hour it would be right on top of us. Already the oddly appealing smell of smoke hung heavy in the air, and the stars were obscured from the haze pouring into the sky.

"We must move quickly, until we are but a mile off the southern cliffs, then take the hill as the flames dance at our feet," said Armon. "We shall hope the giants who remain will not see us through the haze as we pass into the forest on the other side."

We walked on, our pace stronger as the wind increased, and the fire seemed to halve its distance from us in no time at all. Twenty minutes later the flames were closer than we'd hoped they would be.

"We must run!" Armon yelled. He knelt down and instructed me to jump onto the great leather bag on his back and hang on. Then he took Yipes and Murphy on his shoulders and stood erect. John and Odessa were left to run of their own power, goaded on by Armon's colossal steps behind them, like the cracking of a whip at their heels. I was astonished at the size of Armon's back, the breadth of his neck, how high in the air I was, the power of everything about him. It felt as though I were riding a great bull with magnificent strength, that I might be thrown high into the night air and trampled underfoot.

"Follow me the rest of the way," Armon said to our running companions. "We must turn to the hill now and overcome its face. Stay as quiet as you can, muffle your coughing. No matter how tired you become, don't stop until I tell you."

The smoke was much thicker now, coming in waves. A mere fifty yards to our right lay the slithering snake of fire. As it approached us I was surprised by the height of the flames. I had thought they would be only a foot off the ground, but when the wind took them, they darted seven or eight feet up, licking against the night sky.

We had already been moving diagonally against the hill under Armon's lead, and before long we were at its

112

base. I looked back and saw that John and Odessa were right behind us. Ahead lay the most difficult part of the night's journey, and Armon had timed it perfectly. The heat from the fire was growing steadily, and smoke ran in formless white rivers all around us. I kept looking back to see our companions. Finally, about halfway up the side of the hill, the smoke came thick enough between us that I lost sight of them entirely.

"Armon, we've lost them!" I said, and then I looked to my right and found that the fire was no longer a safe distance away. Hidden in the smoke it had crept up on us, the flames dancing now at Armon's leather-clad feet.

Armon darted to the left and continued running up the hill toward the smoke-filled sky. He was moving faster now, bounding in great strides up the hill and moving to the left as he avoided the flames.

"Armon, you're losing them!" I said. "They can't keep up."

But he just kept running, faster and faster, until we reached the edge where the hill topped out, flattened, and tumbled down the other side. He dropped us from his back and shoulders quickly and descended the hill into the smoke from where we had come.

"Keep moving away from the flames and stay just this side of the top," he said as he went. "Don't go down the hill on either side."

At the top of the hill the smoke was not as thick, but breathing was still difficult. Yipes, Murphy, and I stayed in front of the flames as they approached us, slipping down the side of the hill occasionally as we tried to stay off the top and out of sight. I looked down the hill where the smoke was thickest and saw nothing of our two companions.

"I hope they're all right," squeaked Murphy.

Seconds turned to minutes, and we moved at least thirty feet along the edge to stay out of the flames. I glanced up at the sky and realized with some astonishment that a low ceiling of smoke hung all around us in the air, obscuring anything more than a few feet overhead. I was alarmed at how completely the smoke had taken the sky. I also began to wonder how close to the southern cliffs we were, where the hill would taper down and eventually meet with the steep drop-off that ended in jagged rocks and the Lonely Sea below.

While my head was turned toward the cliffs, Odessa came sniffing and pawing at my feet. I knelt down and embraced her around her big bushy neck.

"Armon's got John, right behind me," she said, and no sooner than it was out of her mouth, Armon arrived with John flung over his shoulder. He dropped John to the ground with a thud, and I was happy to see that he was conscious and alert.

"The clouds have moved in," said Armon. "Soon the rain will come and our cover will be lost." He said nothing else, only crouched low and moved to the top of the hill. It was flat for twenty feet, then it dropped off even more steeply than the side we had been on. Looking out over the edge I saw the lights of Castalia's wharf in the distance, but everything else was shrouded in smoke and darkness.

"You must follow me precisely," Armon told us. "Don't veer off my trail to the left or to the right. Hold onto one another so we stay together through the smoke."

Armon began to descend the hill on the opposite side, Yipes and Murphy once again on his shoulders, me holding tightly to the bag on his back. John held Armon by his leather vest, which hung down behind him. With his other hand he grabbed hold of Odessa's mane.

The descent was steep, full of brush and small rocks. I winced every time the pebbles shot out from under Armon's huge feet, fearing the noise would give us away and a monstrous giant would suddenly appear before us. I was glad when we reached the bottom, although the smoke was terribly thick and gray, and I was only able to see a few feet in front of me. My lungs screamed for fresh air, and I could hear myself wheezing as my body tried to adjust. The first drops of rain began to fall and the wind began to swirl around us, the smoke following its master and thinning out as it spun in circles.

"Behold the Valley of Thorns," said Armon. Through the swirling smoke a vast graveyard of poles emerged. "Don't touch anything and move carefully. Delicate wires connect many of the poles, so we must be careful to go around them. The top of every pole is lathered with poison. Imagine this field of venomous tips as you would a labyrinth. Follow me closely. If we leave a trace, they will surely find us."

Armon zigzagged between poles, some of them short and some at my eye level atop Armon's back, all razor sharp at the tip and shining bloodred with poison. I held tightly to the big leather bag and hoped it wouldn't be flung from Armon's back, me with it, impaled onto a pole. The smoke whipped through like a great fog, swirling all around us, and the poles, like hollow bones, stood erect in the thin light of dawn. All the while the rain fell thicker, first only a few drops, then larger and more frequent. Before long the sky would let go all at once, the flames would be snuffed out, and with them the smoke that hid us.

Armon stopped abruptly and remained still and quiet. We were approaching the far edge of the Valley of Thorns, and I could see the outline of trees in the forest before us. But there was something more, movement to the right through what remained of the thin layer of smoke. In the haze of morning my heart pounded against Armon's back, and the sky let go of the rain altogether. The gleaming back of a giant's head appeared, his monstrous, misaligned shoulders swaying to and fro as if working at something in front of him. And then another giant appeared to my right, walking toward the first. This one I saw completely as he passed before us in the murky light only ten feet away, streams of water flowing over his

116

misshapen face, the smell of him so close that even in the cleansing rain I felt my insides quake and sour. He pushed the first giant, and they barked at each other in a language I could not understand. It was guttural and wet and low, as though they were spitting up gobs of phlegm with every word. They marched off into the rain, leaving behind them a tall pole bent a little to the left, as if it were not held in place like the rest.

With the rain coming in sheets and the smoke all but washed away, Armon began to move forward, then pushed John and Odessa into the gloom of the forest. A group of giants was gathering to the right with the two we had seen. Just as they turned to survey the area we occupied, Armon slipped into the trees, taking me with him upon his mighty back.

We remained still a moment, smoke hanging like a deep mist in the trees, and we breathed the forest air. It was a thick section of trees buried in wiry underbrush. I was glad to be on Armon's back, out of reach of the scratches to be had on the forest floor.

"We have yet to pass through the wood, but the haze of smoke will help hide us," Armon said quietly. "Soon we will reach a wooded path that forks off in different directions. One of these forks will lead us to the place where we must hide."

Armon whispered more, telling John and Odessa to watch him and be ready to leave the path and hide in the wood if he should do the same, for the paths were patrolled by Grindall's giants. We moved silently through the gloom and Odessa seemed to struggle the most, her legs tangled often in the deep underbrush. Before long we came upon a winding path. In a place where such death and despair were expected, I was taken aback by the beauty of the simple curves, the smoky mist overhead, light shooting through the clouds that were already moving on and revealing spots of pale blue, the rain now a mist of tiny droplets all around us. Armon set me, Murphy, and Yipes down, and I felt the soft, wet earth beneath my feet. We walked on, curving this way and that, Armon peering forward, then back in search of our enemy.

"Why do they smell so bad?" I whispered. Armon put his finger to his lips and motioned me to be quiet, then he leaned down and whispered back.

"They are rotting from the inside out," he explained. My face soured, and he dropped to one knee, bending low and facing the lot of us.

"My race is all but wiped out," Armon said, and I saw his sadness at admitting he was the last of them. "What remains are not giants. They are transformed, entirely possessed by evil, not a trace of light remains in them. Best we call them ogres from now on, for that is what they have become. I have no kinship with them."

The morning was fully awake now, wet leaves and plants dancing gently in the slight breeze. The sky above was sapphire blue and only a few light clouds remained.

The trees rose high above us on both sides of the path, swaying lazily in the first breath of day.

A racket of noise startled us from behind. I nearly jumped off the path entirely. It was Squire coming to a stop on a tree that lined the path.

"Squire!" whispered Yipes. "Must you be so dramatic?"

But Squire only screeched in reply, an angry look in her eyes.

"Off the path," said Armon, and before I could turn to see him he had taken me by the waist and lifted me off the ground, my face and arms running through thick brush as he carried me away. Squire flew into the air again, and the rest of us crouched in the thicket off the path. All except Murphy, who had found for himself a nut that had fallen from one of the trees. He was absorbed entirely by the crunchy morsel, nibbling aimlessly in the middle of the path, until two dreadful ogres were only a few strides from where he stood. Their shadows overtook Murphy. Looking up, he screamed, ran back and forth as if he'd lost his mind, and then darted up a tree where he looked down on the two ogres in time to see what remained of his breakfast trampled underfoot.

Again there was the unpleasant smell as the ogres passed by, ripe and wet, a loathsome odor of dying flesh raised on the wind and carried to where we crouched motionless in the thicket. They hardly took notice of

Murphy as they moved on. Ahead, where the trail split in two, the ogres went along in opposite directions, one passing deeper into the forest, the other veering off toward the lake.

"Why didn't I think of that?" said Yipes after they had passed. "He'll make a fine lookout from up there — if we can keep him from eating his way through the forest."

And so it was decided that Murphy would remain in the trees above, scouting our way as we passed through the wood. It was really quite beautiful, surprisingly full of birds and other small creatures that scurried away in the brush. The wood ran along the south side of the lake and at a certain point I was able to see through the trees and behold the vast expanse of cobalt blue, the mirror image of Mount Laythen shimmering on its surface. It was unlike anything I could have ever imagined seeing in Bridewell.

For a long while we encountered no other ogres, though Murphy ordered us off the path once when a group of three women passed by in a rickety old cart pulled by a meager-looking horse. I was startled to see other people in the woods, and became newly aware that we were nearing Castalia. I saw the women through the brush, especially the one sitting closest to me on the edge of the cart. She was not pretty, but it seemed as though she might have been once. She appeared tired. Her two companions spoke quietly as they passed, but she remained silent. I rose up in the brush and watched the three dark bonnets on their heads bobbing up and down with the bumps on the trail. Something about the one woman struck me, and I felt as though someone was telling me to remember her face.

We continued on, and soon a new stench was in the air, just as bad as the smell of ogres, yet different, more like rotting garbage. Murphy scampered down a tree, and we all gathered off the trail once more.

There were only four words spoken, but they were words that brought a new feeling of alarm.

"The City of Dogs," said John, and Armon nodded his agreement.

CHAPTER 16

# INTO THE CITY
# OF DOGS

"Just around the bend and in the clearing," said Armon, "the forest thins out and the dumping grounds begin. Within them we shall find the wild dogs, their packs grown larger and more violent with the passing of the years." He paused and sniffed at the air, concentrating, no doubt trying to remember the place as it had been when he had last seen it.

"Take out your weapons and prepare for the worst," he whispered, unsheathing his own massive sword as quietly as he could. Then he eyed Odessa closely, the two of them staring at one another in the stillness.

"You might be of some use to us here," said Armon. "It is possible they might see you as one of their own and let us pass through. But there will be no avoiding them. They know we are here."

We moved down what remained of the path before us, Odessa and Armon striding confidently beside each other at the front. As we came around the one remaining wooded corner the stench almost knocked me off my feet, a gentle breeze carrying with it an omen of what lay ahead.

It was a good deal as I'd expected it would be, a vast expanse of broken-down houses and mountains of flowing debris. Trails shot off in various directions, the hard earth grooved deeply with wheel marks pooling from the rains. Piles of garbage steamed with the morning sun, and the breeze sent a continual flow of pungent new odors over us.

We walked on, following Armon's lead, careful to listen for humans or ogres who might be roaming about. It wasn't long before we were deep in the City of Dogs, and howls could be heard from both near and far. Odessa began to growl as she moved forward with increasing hesitation, her ears pointed and alert for the dogs that might jump out and attack us.

"Where are they, Odessa?" asked Yipes, an arrow pulled and ready to shoot from his small bow.

"They keep moving," she replied, and I translated to the others. "And there is more than one pack, at least two. Both are tracking us and watching one another." Then she stopped entirely and looked back at us. "These are both large packs, fifty or more to be sure."

All at once the sound of growling and barking was all around us, and a moment later we were trapped, one pack of dogs emerging around two garbage heaps to the left of the path, and another pack moving in from the right. They encircled us, row upon row of dogs. They were dripping saliva, some with open wounds and sores around their mouths and noses. Others limped weakly in the row farthest from us.

The group of us came together as the wild dogs inched closer. Running would be futile; it would be what they'd hope we would do, so they could separate us and single us out, take us down at the legs, and rip us to shreds one by one.

"Can't you talk to them, Odessa?" I pleaded. The barking and growling was fierce and I was frightened and shaking. The first row of dogs was just a few feet away. Where the two packs touched, dogs growled and fought one another violently, and I felt it was only a matter of time before we were caught in a storm of teeth and claws as the two packs fought over who would have us as their prize.

A very large and surprisingly healthy-looking black dog with a huge head and a crumpled mane pulled closer to us still, and I took him to be the leader of one of the two packs. Odessa darted between him and me, growling ferociously. The two of them squared off, not attacking but apparently thinking of little else. From the other pack came a similar situation — the largest of the dogs, a brown mixed breed with bushy hair and glaring white teeth, moving out in front to square off with Armon. These were scary creatures, ill with diseases that a single bite could inflict on any one of us.

"You have a choice to make." It was John, his calming voice sending a wave of sniffs and swaying heads across the sea of wild dogs. "We can go to war here in the mire. You will surely overcome us in the end, but not before we slay a good many, if not most, of you. Armon's sword alone will cut a large swath of you to the grave. And who knows, we might even kill each and every one of you before we're through. After all, we have blades and arrows and a giant." John paused and looked around him. "Against a hundred dogs it may not be enough, but it will surely be close."

The black lead dog paced back and forth in confusion, uncertain what to make of this man before him.

"How is it that you speak and we understand?" growled the dog. "Do you hear what I'm saying to you?"

John repeated what was said by the dog word for word, and this further confounded both lead dogs. Confused beyond measure and unsure what to do, the rest of the two packs backed up and waited to see what their respective leaders would do.

"If the two of you will listen to me, I will offer you an alternative that I think you'll agree is to your advantage," said John. He bent down on one knee between the two of them and began to explain who we were and why we had come. He left out many details that were of little consequence. He told them we were here to overthrow Grindall, to free the people from the ogres, and to save a prisoner enslaved in the castle.

"If the two of you can control your packs and use them to help us defeat Grindall and his army of beasts, then I give you my word I will do everything in my power to help you," John concluded.

The mangy brown dog licked at his nose and seemed to contemplate the offer.

"Piggott?" he said, looking at the other leader and questioning his intent. "We have long since chosen our territories and formed our armies. But food runs scarcer by the year and our fighting brings less and less benefit. Soon we'll have to move into the wharf to find food, and this will bring the hammer down on us for good. The giants will come and clear us out one by one until none remain."

The black dog eyed us carefully, standing tall and proud, and I noticed for the first time that his ribs were protruding beneath his gangly hair. How long had he gone without food? I wanted to reach out and pet him, but I feared he might snap at me and dig his teeth into my hand.

"Scroggs," he addressed the brown dog, "could it be that this is the giant who took the last of the stones?" Armon remained quiet, watching in wonder as we communicated with the dogs. To him, Piggott and Scroggs only growled and barked and rolled their heads this way and that. It was a language he could not hope to understand.

I took my Jocasta from its pouch and presented it, glowing even in the full light of day. Piggott and Scroggs backed up a step each, and the rest of the dogs retreated even farther back, some out of sight but for their faces, the rest of their bodies hidden behind broken walls and mounds of rubbish.

"It is indeed the giant Armon, the one they look for day and night," said Scroggs, astonished and trembling. "The end must be nearer than I'd thought."

A great deal of discussion followed, with Piggott and Scroggs fighting over who would hold the highest rank and by what method the packs would merge or otherwise work together. They seemed fiercer than ever in their excitement to overthrow Grindall.

It was decided that we must be hidden, and once again the place would be the clock tower on the far end of the dumping grounds. Scroggs and his pack would roam the north side of the City of Dogs, and Piggott and his brood would roam the south. When the time was right, we would call for them, and as one, the hundred dogs would besiege the castle in the dead of night.

"We will require something in return for our help," said Piggott, and all the dogs from both packs began to whine and bark. "There is a butcher on the wharf. Bring us a hundred slabs of fresh meat and we will fight to the death. These beasts deserve one good meal in their lives, and I aim to give it to them."

I looked out upon the two packs. With the ominous growling and barking at bay they were a sad lot indeed. Many of them were large but oddly frail and meek, and most were quite clearly ill. I felt sorry for them then, and though I wished I could save them all, I knew that victory against Grindall would mean little for these creatures. Their lives were marked for a death that would come sooner rather than later. Scroggs and Piggott knew this, and maybe that's why they so willingly joined us in our quest. A heroic end by the knife was a better end than the one both packs faced. They hated Grindall and the ogres and their evil ways, and this was the chance to destroy them, to be of some great purpose at the very end.

"John and I can do it," I said. "We'll get you your meal, more if we can hold it."

The packs stayed to their sides while Scroggs and Piggott led us deeper still into the City of Dogs on our way to the clock tower. There was only one thing more that we lacked, something upon which our ability to succeed almost entirely depended. What we needed was Castalians, and we needed a great many of them.

# CHAPTER 17

# THE WHARF

The clock tower was just as I'd imagined it when I'd heard the story. It looked mysterious sitting alone among weeds and debris, as though secret things had taken place there in the distant past. It was round and made of stone, lined with ivy, and looked very old. I immediately wanted to touch it and feel something of the place where Laura and Catherine had hidden.

"It's fantastic," I said, looking up at John in the cooling night air. He only nodded, lost in his thoughts of this place in the same way I was.

Both our faces were shrouded by hoods fashioned from blankets. It was common for Castalia's peasants to wear a throw this way, and it helped to make us feel more as though we would not be noticed or picked out as outsiders if we encountered anyone. The rest of our attire was in keeping with that of a commoner; everything we wore was dirty and tattered from our journey, John with his shabby tunic, me with an earth-brown tunic frayed at the ankles and an old pair of weathered leather sandals.

We had left everyone else behind in the clock tower to begin planning how we might rescue Catherine and rid Castalia of Grindall and the ogres. In the tower it was stuffy and hot, and I was glad to be free of it. Even still, the open air of the City of Dogs smelled as though it could be cut like a block of cheese. I longed to be near the lake where the air would smell fresh and clean.

Armon had already thought a great deal about how best to go about our business with Grindall. He had explained in detail how we should approach the wharf without being seen and how to blend in should someone engage us. Both John and I carried our leather satchels on our backs. They were empty, but we hoped to return to the clock tower with as much meat as we could put in them.

"The butcher, he usually takes in three or four pigs in the morning," said Piggott, who was scouting just ahead of us, leading us quietly to the edge of the wharf where he would wait for our return. "In the back of the shop he cures the ham and boils the bones. It is there where you will find what we want. The hams will be heavy, but you can manage it. You can cut them up in the clock tower."

Piggott continued on, John and I following, until we reached the last of the broken-down buildings and piles of trash. Before us lay an open stretch of field. Beyond the field emerged the shimmering edge of the lake, its surface a liquid sea of black, marked by reflections grasped from the stars and the moon above.

"If you cross the field here and stay along the lake, you will find the wharf," said Piggott. He sat down and scratched vigorously against the side of his head. "This stretch is not patrolled by giants, only by humans. They will not be looking for intruders, since no one ever comes.

They look only for those trying to escape. But even these are so few that the guards mostly sleep or gamble in the night. If you are careful you should have no trouble entering the wharf. Getting out could prove a bigger challenge, but if you're watchful and quiet you will get past."

Before our departure, Armon was careful to explain that on the wharf, darkness meant few people would be out and about. We would see occasional guards and ogres, and we might see washmaids dumping dirty water or men hauling out debris, but the streets would be mostly barren until morning.

John was first to venture out into the open of the field; I followed with some hesitation, wishing for once that I might stay in the squalid safety of the City of Dogs. It was not far to the edge of the lake, and as we approached, the air cooled and the night felt calm and peaceful. The sound of water lapping lazily on the rocks soothed my frazzled spirit, and for a moment I was taken back home behind my desk again, bored but happy and safe.

We walked quickly along the water, following it toward the dim lights not far in the distance. I heard voices carried over the lake, and began to wonder who we might encounter and what they might be doing. Two men, probably guards, walked along the lake as we did, making their way toward us, each with a torch in hand. John took my hand and we darted out into the field, then lay perfectly still on the ground in the brush and waited.

The men came only a little farther, then turned back to the wharf without reaching us, talking peaceably as they went.

We rose and followed well behind them until they disappeared around a corner and we stood at the edge of the wharf where houses began to appear. It was nearing eleven o'clock in the evening, and as Armon had suspected, the cobblestone streets were deserted.

Even in the darkness it was clear that the wharf was a dirty place. The houses and the fronts of the small buildings were made of whitewashed stone and wood, but these were simple structures lacking any charm or character, and many were marked with broken facades and crumbling corners. The street was made of small cobblestones, much smaller than the ones at home, and the recent rain had left many of the stones covered with mud. A stone wall, three feet high, ran along the lake side of the wharf, and every twenty feet an opening appeared that led down to the water's edge.

"What shall we do?" I asked.

John motioned me forward and we walked along the edge of the wall until we reached an opening. Then we crossed through the opening and crouched down behind the wall, moving quietly along the lake. Beneath our feet were clumps of brush, pebbles, and rocks, but we were hidden by the little wall along the lake. We passed a group of guards throwing dice and a man rolling a noisy cart down the cobbled street. Lamps lit the night along the street, but we were able to move ahead without notice in the relative darkness next to the lake.

A while later we came upon a group of women standing next to the wall. They were washing clothes and talking quietly. One of them walked through the opening and poured dirty water into the lake, then took her wooden bucket and filled it once again. She wore a blue bonnet, as did the rest of them, and as she turned to go back to her work I saw that she had the same expression as the woman I'd seen passing through the City of Dogs earlier in the day. She was sad and tired, going through her motions as if she were only half-awake.

She rejoined her companions, and the four of them worked and talked quietly. We would have to cross over into the street and pass them in the open to find the butcher's shop. The two of us backtracked and emerged where the light was scarce. We covered our faces and looked down, then walked along the street toward the women in blue bonnets. I could hear another cart rolling down a side street and the guttural voice of an ogre somewhere behind us. The voice was far enough off that I couldn't tell for sure where it had come from as the sound bounced off the lake. We quickened our pace and soon enough we were nearing the women, the sound of wet clothing slapping against soapy stones and the sharp, white smell of detergent hanging in the air.

I kept on with John and listened as the women stopped their work and the street became quiet. Then we passed in front of them, my eyes downcast and watching as the small cobblestones rushed by beneath my feet.

"You should not be about at this hour," came a voice, quiet but firm. "Have you some work you are attending to?"

When I glanced up I saw that it was the woman from the forest, the quiet one on the cart whose face I couldn't forget. How could we meet twice by chance in such a small window of time? I wondered if Elyon was indeed pulling on strings from within the Tenth City, moving people around so they might encounter one another. I instinctively placed my hand over the leather pouch holding my Jocasta, then stopped on the street even as John tried to pull me forward.

I had been surrounded by men my whole life, and the journey to Castalia, with the mostly silent exception of Odessa, had been no different. This was a reality that did not bother me in the least — I lived in what often felt like a man's world, and I'd come to accept this fact and even enjoy my unique place in it. But there was something about this woman's face and the way she'd spoken to us. I understood her in a way John did not. I felt a hidden hope in her questioning — a hope that John and I might be something more than two peasants wandering in the night.

"You work late tonight," I said, still not turning to face her, but letting her know that I was a girl.

"We are behind on the washing, and so we work," answered the woman, the others whispering beside her. The woman's tone remained quiet and measured, as if speaking was something she did only when necessary. "That is the way of things in Castalia. You know this." She was probing me, looking for more.

John pulled on my tunic once again, and this time I took his hand and gently pushed it away. Then I looked up, full into the faces of the four women, and pulled the covering off my head, letting it rest around my shoulders.

"We are not from here," I said, a cold wave of fright washing over me as the words tumbled out of my mouth. There was a moment of silence, and then I reached out my hand and softly touched the closest woman on the arm. "We have come to help you."

And there it was, out in the open. Everything we had risked and all that we hoped for hung in the wind. They could scream for help, and we would be captured and tortured in Grindall's dungeon. All would be lost. Abaddon would gather the stones and Elyon would be overcome.

The voice of the ogre was coming closer, moving in from a side street, wheezing and spitting, his huge feet clomping along the earth as he came.

"The enemy is upon us. What do you say?" I asked. The woman looked at her companions and seemed to consider if any of them were about to give us away. John began tugging at me again, pulling me down the street against my will.

"Pack up your things and get back to the house," the woman said. The other three smiled broadly and started to move. The woman reached out her hand to me. I looked at John and he hesitated, then nodded his cautious approval. The moment I took her hand the three of us were racing across the street, and soon we had vanished in the maze of narrow streets, turning first this way and then that. She said nothing as we went. This was not the quiet woman I'd seen in the forest on the cart or at the wharf doing the washing. She was energized, alert, and purposeful.

Somewhere in the twists and turns along the wharf she stopped and peered around a blind corner. Here she squeezed my hand harder and whispered in my ear.

"Do not be afraid," she said, and then she motioned for me to look around the edge with her. Twenty yards off was a high wall made of stone, and within it was fashioned a massive gate of iron. Before the gate stood two ogres armed with enormous swords. Beyond the gate was a dark path, and beyond the path a series of torches that climbed into the darkness. Against the night was a single spire, rising into the stars, a threatening shadow invading the sky.

"It's the Dark Tower," she whispered. "Grindall's castle."

"Why did you bring us here?" I said, unsure as we stood so close to the enemy. She held my hand tighter still. One pull and it would be over; I would be out in the open and helpless.

She turned to both of us, her former beauty clear to me even in the darkness. Though beaten down and aged by poverty, she had a perfect face, and the tears in her eyes made me want to rescue her more than anything I'd ever wanted before.

"He is a wicked man, led by wicked forces," she whispered, her voice trembling with emotion. "No one knows the things that happen in the Dark Tower, only that these things are evil."

She paused and looked around the corner once again, then back at us. "The giants grow angrier and more violent by the day. They grow more ill, more rotten. And Grindall grows more impatient for whatever it is he is searching for. It consumes him."

I looked her squarely in the face, my own voice surprisingly firm and reassuring as I spoke. "I know what it is he searches for, and why," I said, no longer afraid of what I might reveal.

"So do I," said the woman, and then she winked at me and smiled coyly for a moment. I could not help but return the smile at seeing the hope in her face.

"We should go," said John, his hand firmly gripping the sword he had kept hidden, his eyes darting this way and that, searching for trouble from where it might come.

The woman spun me around, and again we were

whipping down the streets back toward the water's edge. While we ran I told her my name and John's, and she told us hers was Margaret. I couldn't say whether Margaret was taking us on the same route or a different one — the narrow streets and passages wound in every direction and the facades all looked familiar, but then everything was a slum built of stone and wood and to see one building was to see them all.

We came to a wooden door with a round knocker shaped like a horseshoe. Margaret took the knocker in her fingers and rapped three times, a thick wooden sound echoing down the street. A moment later the entrance creaked open. We crept inside, and the door was shut and locked behind us.

# CHAPTER 18

# BALMORAL

There was a fire burning. A few small candles — two of them on a big old table, another one melting on a pile of wood in a corner — also added to the dim light in the small room. A little girl sat on the floor, playing with onion peels dropped from her mother's lap. The girl was carefully tearing the papery peels into dolls and clothing for them to wear. She and her mother stopped what they were doing and stared at us, the girl clinging to her mother's leg, the mother gaping at the sight of us.

There was also a man in the room, skinny with a bushy black beard. He stood next to the fire with a poker in his hand. It was he who had opened the door, after which he had stared in disbelief at Margaret for bringing us. He had big eyes, sallow cheeks, and a mop of dark hair on top of his head.

To our right were the other three women we had seen by the lake. One was washing a brown plate in a wooden barrel, another was plucking the feathers off a small bird, and the third was hanging wet clothing on a wire that passed to the side of the fireplace. A heavy oblong table, marred with age, sat in the very center of the room, strewn with roots and potatoes, wooden dishes and pitchers. Two long, thick benches sat along the table, and

Margaret, who had gone rather pale, motioned for John and me to sit on one of them; then she went over to the man, and the two of them whispered while everyone else in the room pretended to go back to what he or she had been doing.

"I like your dolls," I said to the girl. She seemed the easiest one to approach, even with the mother towering above her. "I never thought of making them that way. You must be a clever girl."

She beamed at me, and then looked at her mother as if to say, "She's nice, may I play with her?" Before she got her answer, the man at the fire moved to the center of the room and looked at us with a wary eye.

"My name is Balmoral and this is my home." He waved his hand around the room in a grand gesture. "Grindall's had us working until after dark most nights, so dinner's come late indeed. You're welcome to stay as long as you like, and if you haven't eaten, we'll have a kettle of onion and magpie soup within the hour."

He placed his hand to the side of his mouth and leaned closer, then whispered, "She's mostly onion and water, but you'll get a nibble of meat here and there if you're at the front of the line." And then he smiled just a little, and I could see that he was a hospitable sort, glad of the unexpected company, curious about the reason for our visit.

"Enid, take your wash bucket and walk down to the lake and back. Make sure nobody saw these two come in."

A young woman, one of the three from before, dashed across the room, picked up an old wooden bucket, and moved toward the door. Margaret removed the wood plank that barred the door and opened it. When Enid had gone, Margaret pushed the door shut and put the plank back on its iron claws, locking us in once again.

When the door was shut I began thinking about the boiled magpie. This, mixed with the strong smell of onions and body odors, made me put my hand over my mouth and lower my head. The whole world smelled thick and pasty. I wished I could get back out in the open air next to the lake and breathe.

"I know, I know. The onions are a bit ripe. Not so ripe as the lot of us, though, don't you think?" Balmoral burst out laughing, and I could see that one of his front teeth was missing. The women in the room seemed to think him quite funny, and they began to laugh along with him. Soon enough I was laughing, too. Even John, still nervous about our predicament, expressed some amusement as he smiled and looked around the room.

"You'll find we're a happy bunch in the nighttime," continued Balmoral, bringing himself under control with a wipe of a tear from his eye and a dying spasm of chuckles. "We've not much to live for, but we have one another and our privacy when the sun goes down. We live as best we can amid the reign of Grindall."

The man walked back over to the fire and poked it with his gaff. Sparks flew up and lit the room for an instant, and then Balmoral put his finger in the black kettle that hung over the fire and pulled his hand away quickly.

"I do believe we're ready for those onions." He wiped his fingers along the brown sleeve of his tunic, then he looked affectionately at the woman peeling onions.

"This here's my wife, Mary," he said, and as he continued I learned that the young girl making onion paper dolls was Julia, his daughter. Margaret was his younger sister by two years, and the other women were Gwen, Rose, and the recently departed Enid. When he finished introducing these last ladies he added, "Them three's widows." Then he bowed reverently, rose, and looked again at them.

"An awful sickness ran through the place a year ago and took one in ten of us." Balmoral was momentarily downcast; clearly some of those who had died had been his friends, and he missed them. But he wasted little time on the sadness of the past, his mood brightening a moment later.

"Well then, if what Margaret tells me is true, we've got a bit of talking to do, haven't we?" he said. Mary stood behind him, dumping onions into the pot with a wet plop.

The next hour passed quickly as John and I told the Castalians everything we knew. We started with Warvold's story and our journey, then the legends of Elyon and Abaddon, and finally our plans to rescue

Renny and overthrow Grindall. All the while Balmoral drank ale and stood by the fire, occasionally taking a large wooden spoon to sample the soup. He was very inquisitive and cheerful as we spoke. "Ogres you call 'em?" "You say his name was Warvold?" "You have a stone, one of the special stones?" — on and on he went with his questions as we waited for the soup to be finished.

Eventually Balmoral took the big black pot from where it hung over the fire and placed it on the stone floor before him.

"The thing about the giants — the ogres — they weren't so bad before they . . . well, I assume you've seen 'em?" Balmoral asked as he looked around the room. John told him the last detail he needed to know, that we had on our side the last of the giants, a true giant, one not possessed by Abaddon, one who would fight to the death to free Castalia.

This bit of information seemed of particular interest to Balmoral. As he scooped up bowls of steaming soup, he looked at John with a seriousness I had not yet seen in him.

"Then it's true," he said, a half-filled bowl of soup in one hand. "The legend comes to pass on this very night."

The flickering light danced in the whites of his enormous, sunken eyes, and Balmoral stared off into the fire for a long moment of contemplation, the big wooden spoon dripping watery soup into the kettle. Then he seemed to awaken from his trance and began pouring more bowls of soup.

143

We gathered around the table, little Julia making sure to find a spot next to me. I was surprised to hear them offer a prayer to Elyon, lifting up their hands in the air and thanking him, asking for his return. They did not plead for their freedom or cry out in anguish. Instead they were thankful for a watery bowl of magpie soup. When the prayer was finished they ate slowly, drank their ale, and smiled often. I tickled Julia in the ribs and made her jump; she laughed and leaned her head against my arm, and as we played at big and little sister, I ventured a question to the Castalians.

"You believe Elyon is real?"

Balmoral started to answer, but Margaret gently touched his forearm and offered her thoughts instead.

"Thousands have suffered and died to build that castle of beasts," she said, wiping her mouth with the flap of her apron, her voice shaking as it had before. "We have been in the midst of an immense evil for a very long time, and no one has come to help us. But, in its way, the evil has been a comfort, as if by its very presence we know the stories that have been passed on are true. Elyon is among us, close by, waiting in the shadows, until the cruelty runs its course and he returns to claim us."

Even in the midst of her affecting answer I remained unsatisfied. "Yes . . . but how do you know he will return?" I asked. "He's been away an awfully long time. Long enough that many from where I come don't remember him at all."

Margaret raised her spoon full of broth and tipped it, the beads of liquid dripping back into her bowl.

"Where does the water come from? Who makes this air I breathe in and breathe out? I don't know how these things are made, and yet I live."

She paused then, thinking, before she continued:

"Evil rules my people, but the giants become monsters just as the stories said they would. And you — you come with the last of the stones around your neck, just as the ancient stories say. And where do these stories come from? Either they are a wicked trick of Abaddon or they are the truth. I choose to believe they are the truth. The time has come for Abaddon to fall, for Elyon to return."

"They can be killed, you know," said Balmoral, smacking his lips between sips of broth. I looked at him, not immediately understanding what he meant. "The ogres, they can be killed." He took another big slurp of soup and a slug from his big metal pint of ale. "Just need to put your blade in the right spot. Only problem is the spot is a bit difficult to get at, since it's at the top of their heads."

I took a mouthful of my own soup, which was not as bad as I feared it might be. Mary had added wildflower, cypress root, and ginger, and I found myself enjoying the sharp flavor of the onions despite the occasional chewy bit of magpie.

"They wear chain mail at their chest and back under all that wretched black clothing, metal plates over the shoulders, legs, and neck," Balmoral continued. "They also have helmets, but their sorry heads are so full of open sores and scabs they can't stand to wear 'em. I've seen an ogre up close when one of 'em was dunking his head into a vat of water. I tell you, it's a bloody mess. That's where the damage is the greatest, on top of their heads. It's just a big open wound up there; near drives them crazy with anger."

He took three more spoonfuls of soup and slurped them loudly before looking up from his bowl to notice we were all staring at him. His bulging, comical eyes darted to and fro, a drop of slippery broth sliding down his hairy chin.

"Oh, yes, a blade in the top of the head would do it, I think. I'm almost sure it would," he said, and then, sensing he had for himself an audience, he went on. "I have a thought that might clarify things a bit more, if you like."

Seeing no objections, Balmoral looked longingly at his half-eaten bowl of broth, set aside his wooden spoon, and ran a ragged sleeve across his mouth.

"The thing you must never forget is the order in which things were made," he began. I was already confused, and Balmoral could tell. He ran his hand over his bearded face and started again.

"If Elyon really did create everything from the start, he would have special knowledge no one else would have. We didn't show up until quite a long while after the Seraphs and the giants and The Land of Elyon itself, so

146

Elyon certainly knows more about us than we know even about ourselves. But wouldn't that also be true of other things he created, especially the first things?"

Balmoral was beginning to sound wiser than I'd expected when I'd set eyes on him.

"On Abaddon's side are Grindall and the ogres; these are the things of evil, things like rage, malice, and deceit. But we cast our lot on a different side, a side controlled by Elyon, who is just, wise, and kind."

Balmoral looked once again at his bowl, was overcome with hunger, and lifted it to his mouth, neglecting the spoon entirely as he gulped down the last of what remained.

"Ahhhh. So much more pleasant to talk on a full stomach, don't you think?" He picked up his mug of ale, took a mighty swig, and belched outrageously. Then he continued with his thoughts.

"Now, from where we're sitting, Grindall and the ogres look insurmountable. It seems as though taking on such a monstrous foe would be foolhardy. But let me go back to my original statement and show you why things may not be entirely as they seem."

He looked around the room, giving pause to the moment, while Julia squeezed my hand and leaned yet closer to my lap.

"The thing you must never forget is the order in which things were made," he repeated. "For you see, Elyon created not only The Land of Elyon and people like you and me. A long time ago he also created Abaddon, and who is to say that when he did he might not have done something unexpected?"

Balmoral lowered his voice almost to a whisper.

"In the same way that you or I might form a bit of clay into a figure in our hands, Elyon made Abaddon as the brightest of the Seraphs — as a friend and a helper. If Elyon was wise and planned ahead — which I must assume he did — isn't it possible that he planned for the unlikely event that things might spin terribly out of control? That this once great friend of Elyon might turn on him?"

Balmoral got up from his seat and stood in front of the fire, the light dancing off his silhouette. He took a worn old pipe from the charred mantel and lit it with a stick dipped into the fire. Looking longingly around the room, he blew a puff of smoke up over his head.

"Here we stand," he continued, "toe to toe against Grindall and a host of beastly giants ready to dash out our brains. And yet there may still be hope. What if Elyon set a trap that would only be sprung if Abaddon turned on him? I believe that is precisely what has happened, and this has given us the advantage we were meant to have."

We were all riveted by what Balmoral was saying. He was a wise man in peasants' garments, a tooth missing and stinking of sweat, but full of ideas and enthusiasm.

"When Abaddon turned the black swarm on the giants he was lost in a mad rage, and in his cruelty he took all the evil at his disposal and put it into the most power-ful creatures he could find. The giants were actually kind in the beginning, but now that they are possessed by Abaddon, what remains in them is only malice, hate, and blind fury."

We were getting to the end of his tale, and he rushed to the finish from his place next to the fire.

"Ahhhh, but the trap has sprung! The giants cannot contain such evil without having the evil pour from them. It's too great a darkness for their bodies to hold, and so they are teeming with sores, especially upon the head, where it dances like a fire in their brains.

"The last of the story is not known — it was not revealed to us or to Abaddon. We stand at the edge of what our world was and what it will become. If we do not defeat the ogres and Grindall here and now, Abaddon will spread his sickness like a plague across the land, bringing evil wherever he goes, and his goal will be simple — to destroy all of humankind and drive Elyon out of the Tenth City. Only then will Abaddon's work be complete."

"You speak like a man I once knew, a very wise man," I said, thinking Balmoral sounded something like Warvold in his more reflective moments.

"I believe that Abaddon has fallen into the trap, a trap that makes his mighty army vulnerable to a strike. With a bit of planning I think we can defeat the ogres, all but the ten who guard the Dark Tower. I'm afraid those might be a bit of a problem."

"So there are eighty-eight outside the castle and ten inside?" John asked.

"That's right. And we're quite sure where most of the eighty-eight are at any given moment." It was Margaret, speaking out after a long silence. "They run in two shifts, one by day and one by night, and they switch over at dawn and dusk," she continued. "There are usually forty-four that move about at night, forty-four when it's light outside. There are fifteen along the Valley of Thorns, another ten patrolling the forest, and three along the cliffs at the sea; on the wharf are ten more making their rounds, two watch the gate leading up to the tower, and four stand guard around the base of the Dark Tower itself."

"And the sleeping giants?" asked John.

"There is a barracks next to the Dark Tower, down by the lake," said Margaret. "I can only imagine what an awful place it must be. The stench alone is surely wretched beyond imagination."

"There is yet another problem we have neglected to mention," said Balmoral. He turned and grabbed hold of a stone in the mantel of the fireplace, pulled it out, and reached inside. When his hand came out it held what one might call a short sword, about a foot long with a primitive wooden handle.

"This would be one of only a very few fighting blades we have among us in Castalia. Grindall does not stand for a weapon of any kind in the hands of a peasant, and he's been diligent about making sure there are none to be had.

150

We have no armor, no helmets, few swords, and certainly no bows and arrows. What we have is hidden away, and I don't think it numbers more than a few dozen shabby blades."

As Balmoral went on, we discovered there were ways to get hold of things quickly that could be used as weapons, things like axes and small knives used for various tasks on the wharf, but these were few in number and our lack of protective armor remained a problem. We were nearly weaponless with no shields for defense. Our enemy, full of anger and three times the size of a full-grown man, had an almost impossible advantage. It was a hopeless situation.

Just then, a frantic knock came at the door. Margaret was nearest to the entrance and, after looking through the peephole, removed the plank. To our surprise, Enid burst into the room, pushing the door closed behind her. Shaking, she fumbled with the plank and dropped it, then Margaret helped her secure it over the door once more.

Enid turned to us, out of breath, and stammered, "Someone has seen them! The giants are going from door to door looking for intruders on the wharf!"

## CHAPTER 19

# THE ⊙GRE

We looked at one another for a brief, still moment, faint sounds from the fireplace popping gently through the room. Then there was a terrible, loud bang on the door. Julia buried her head in my arm and I held her close.

"Ogre!" Balmoral whispered. He dropped his pipe where he stood, bound for the table, and grabbed hold of his daughter, then thrust the girl into her mother's arms.

"To the back of the room with you, and cover the poor child's eyes," he said. All of the women obeyed except me. I rose from the table and stood with John in the center of the room. Again there was a pounding at the door, this time so loud and violent the very walls shook and sparks flew up into the chimney.

"Margaret! Come quickly," said Balmoral. "You unhitch the door then run for the back of the room. I'm going for the rooftops to see if I can get a shot at him from above." He was gone into a dark corner of the room and up a makeshift ladder before anyone could stop him, swinging open a trapdoor and disappearing outside.

Margaret was so frightened she could hardly speak. She slowly inched her way toward the door, but when it was pounded again so hard it almost fell off the hinges and into the room, she backed away into the shadows where the others sat trembling against the wall. I looked at John.

"Do you want me to open it?" I asked, my hands shaking as I grabbed an iron and walked toward the entryway. John nodded his approval, holding his small sword out into the air in front of him. A moment later I stood at the door and slid the plank free. There was a final crash against the door and it flew open, the ogre's massive arm throwing me to the floor in the center of the room.

He was so big, so horrible — the small space of the home seemed to magnify everything about him. His huge swollen head, the shoulders hunched over, the awful smell of his rotting body. The women were screaming as he swung wildly around the room, grunting until he stood staring at me, dripping thick green and red from his lower lip. John leaped onto the table and stood with his sword drawn to protect me. As the beast turned to him, I crawled through his enormous legs to safety.

With John on top of the table, he and the ogre were almost the same height. The ogre unsheathed his giant sword and held it out toward John's. It was as though John were holding a butter knife, and from where I lay in the room I knew he had no chance of escape.

"Run for the door, Alexa! Take the women and the child with you. Get them out of here while I have his attention!"

It was a brave thing to ask, knowing he could never escape from the room alive on his own. He was my protector, my friend. I couldn't bear the idea of letting him go.

Just then a guttural noise from outside the room escaped into the night air.

"Aaaaarggghhh!"

Any hope I'd had was taken away completely as I waited for more ogres to enter the room. I clutched my Jocasta and whispered a desperate plea. *"Where are you, Elyon? Will you help us?"*

The ogre turned away from John and in one stride was at the doorjamb. When he turned John jumped from the table and lunged at the beast from behind. There was a loud clang as his blade struck armor. I was overcome with fear, cowering in the dark recesses of the room, watching in frozen horror as the ogre stepped closer to my friend.

"Run, Alexa! You must escape!" John yelled. The ogre took one swing at him — not with the sword, but with his huge hand. I watched with horror as John was thrown into the wall with terrible force. His body fell, slumped against the wall, to the ground.

The ogre turned in our direction and sniffed the air as if he'd smelled something he was looking for. His eyes fell on the leather pouch around my neck.

"Aaaaarggghhh!"

It was the noise from outside the door once more, more ghastly than the last time we'd heard it. I felt certain this was where my life and the adventure would end, torn to pieces by two ogres in a peasant's hovel.

The ogre heard the noise and returned to the door-jamb, lowering his gruesome head to get out. He peered from side to side, then made a terrible sound and began staggering to and fro, ducking his head back into the room. He turned in our direction, and there before us was the wooden handle of a blade sticking out of the top of the ogre's head.

The ogre teetered drunkenly, his eyes bulging and wild, and dropped his huge sword with a loud clang. One of his feet stepped into the fire, sparks igniting up his leg. Then the ogre fell over the table and onto the stone floor in a smelly heap. Balmoral jumped down off the roof and landed in the doorway. With a look of satisfaction on his face, he strode into the room, dusted himself off, and stood over the giant.

"You see there, I told you it would work," Balmoral said, a wide smile across his face. I stood up next to Balmoral and looked at the ogre.

At first the beast lay perfectly still. I could hear the faint, disgusting sound of his insides squishing free, the sound of death permeating the room. But then one of his long arms swept quickly out along the floor and the extended fingers caught hold of me at the ankle and jerked me off my feet in one powerful motion. I kicked with my free leg and Balmoral struck the terrible beast over and over again with his bare fists. The ogre let go of my leg for an instant and then the huge hand was across my chest, wrapping tightly around the leather pouch that held my Jocasta. Balmoral kept on swinging at the ogre with little effect. The ogre seemed to be entirely dead but for its one hand holding tightly to what it had found.

"Out of the way!" It was John, advancing across the room, sword in hand. He swung the sword down on the ogre's arm again and again, but it was like trying to cut through inches of worn leather. As I lay there I looked at the ogre's face, and for a brief moment he opened his eyes and saw John standing over him. The sight of John swinging away with the sword seemed to bring forth some final bit of rage stored up in the ogre. Faster than I thought possible, the hand let go of the Jocasta and the arm shot up. I was free, but the ogre had taken hold of John's neck and pulled him down to the floor.

I scurried away, screaming for Balmoral to do something. John Christopher's eyes caught mine then, and though I expected to see fear, he only looked at me as he always had — peaceful, a faint smile, as if he were doing just the thing he had come to do. Then his eyes closed and everything was quiet but for the faint crying of the women and the child in the room.

I sat stunned, unable to believe what had happened. Balmoral lunged for the blade in the ogre's head and pressed it deeper. I knew I shouldn't do it, but for some reason I moved closer to John, not caring whether or not the ogre would come alive again. I touched John's face, and then I did the only thing I could think of that made any sense at all. I placed both my hands on the pouch around his neck, opened it, and took out the glowing blue Jocasta. The ogre did not stir, all the life now passed out of him.

I held the blue stone in the faint light of the room and listened to Julia whimpering in the corner. The Jocasta was still throbbing, its light like a dying heart beating its last. I walked over to Julia and handed it to her, watching as she took it. She held it in her little hand and it beat three more times. *Boom, boom, boom.* The last of the watery blue light faded away, and I knew for certain that John Christopher was no longer among us.

The last Jocasta hung around my neck. All the rest were gone forever.

# CHAPTER 20

# THE SECRET IN ARMON'S LEATHER BAG

The whole world seemed to shrink to the one fact: John was dead. I wanted time to stop. I wanted everything to stop. I wanted simply to stay in the same place and mourn my friend's death. But everything kept moving as it always does. I was still alive, and I was still involved in things that wouldn't wait for my needs to be met. The night was late, and I knew I had to gather my things and go.

Balmoral had visited with his friend the butcher and said what needed to be said in order to fill both packs with meat. Hearing of our terrible night and our plans to help liberate Castalia, the butcher had even gone to the trouble of slicing the meat into single portions.

I kissed Julia on the head and we embraced, and I told her to be ready. I promised things were going to get better very soon. Then Balmoral and Margaret called me to the door and it shut behind us, the cool night air a welcome relief from the ghastly scene inside.

"There was nothing you or anyone else could have

done," Balmoral told me. "The ogre had him, and no amount of force was going to set your friend free."

He was carrying one of the packs full of meat and would have carried both had I not insisted on taking the second. I heard his words but didn't listen, my mind racing back to the room where I'd sat over John and wept. I had pulled the terrible dead hand off his throat and tried my best to say good-bye. We would bring him back to Bridewell, but for now I had to leave.

"Something is different," I said. Margaret took hold of my hand and tried to comfort me, said something about how things were going to change, that John's death would not be in vain.

"That's not what I meant," I said. "I feel something I haven't felt before. It started the moment John's Jocasta faded away."

"What do you feel?" asked Balmoral.

And then a long silence followed by words I had never been surer of.

"Elyon is near. It's as if I feel his very presence hanging around my neck."

It was the most unusual feeling, both comforting and frightening at the same time. I felt as though some new presence had moved suddenly closer, a wonderful presence, but a dangerous one as well.

We walked a while more in silence and arrived at the edge of the wharf, the two guards aware of our presence.

As if on cue, they stepped aside, bowed graciously in Balmoral's direction, and let us pass into the night without a word. I looked at Balmoral, and he whispered, "They may work for Grindall, but they are still Castalians." Then he winked at me and we continued on in silence until we reached the edge of the trees, where Piggott stood waiting. As I had expected, he was full of questions. "Who are these people?" "Where is John?" "What took so long?" "Did you get the meat?" I waved him off with my hand and told him he would have to wait for answers until we reached the clock tower. As we entered the forest, Margaret took hold of my hand.

"Balmoral will go with you and meet with Armon," she said, "but I must return home and help clean up before dawn. We have but a few precious hours before light. Before night sets again we must be ready to strike if we are to catch Grindall unaware."

"She's right," said Balmoral. "Either we mobilize and attempt a strike tomorrow night, or we risk losing our advantage. Already an ogre is dead, and he will be missed."

Margaret hugged me, and I think if not for the work I knew lay ahead, I would have wept and wept in her arms. Instead I made it a quick encounter, turned, and left her standing at the edge of the wood.

Before long we arrived and entered the clock tower where we met Murphy and Yipes. We left the two heavy packs of meat in the lower chamber for Piggott and

Scroggs to distribute as they pleased, then we ascended the ladder, Murphy on my shoulder squeaking question after question.

The upper room of the clock tower, suffused with gray light, held the soft glow of night like a cup of warm milk. As soon as I was all the way up the ladder and in the room, I slumped over in a corner, completely exhausted, and I cried uncontrollably. My friend was gone forever, the stress of what remained of our task was heavy on my mind, and I longed for the many comforts of home. The adventure had become something more, something that was no longer fanciful. Already a great cost had been paid, and as I wept, I felt certain much more would be paid before we were through. I looked up to see silent faces all around me, filled with concern, and I was able to compose myself enough to tell them who Balmoral was and let him give the account of the evening.

"It will have to be quick. We've absolutely no time to waste," he said, and then he proceeded to tell them all about our encounter with the ogre, about the weaknesses we had discovered in their defense, and about the death of John.

Yipes gasped when he heard the news, while Murphy came over and curled into a ball in my lap — a perfect, silent gesture. Armon remained still, closed his eyes, and lowered his head. Odessa remained standing and slowly lowered her head, too, until her nose hung only inches from the floor.

"He was brave, very brave," said Balmoral. "He stood his ground to protect the innocent, and if we win the fight before us, his death will forever be remembered as the beginning of the end of the reign of Grindall."

Armon raised his head, looked Balmoral squarely in the face, and questioned him.

"What powers do you have to rally your people?"

"If Grindall allowed a leader among us, I would be that leader," said Balmoral. I looked at this simple, feeble man, and I was stunned. All the while I'd been in the presence of the true ruler of the Castalians, and I'd thought him nothing more than a broken man with some fanciful ideas.

"I can have two hundred men ready to fight by nightfall the next, but our weaponry is primitive — stones, a few dozen knives, no armor to speak of. The fifty Castalian guards who work for Grindall don't even have swords. They have only horns to blow when trouble is afoot, and then the ogres come running. It is a problem for which I have no answer."

Armon looked long and hard at Balmoral, and though he could not stand upright in the space, he did get up on one knee.

"I don't think that will be such a problem," he said. Then he took hold of the massive bag he'd been carrying since we'd met him, untied the rope at the top, and poured the contents into the middle of the room. Sword after sword fell forth. Chain mail, shields, bows, and arrows all tumbled onto the floor. The pack seemed to hold an endless array of armament. It must have weighed hundreds of pounds, and I was newly amazed by Armon's superhuman strength. Balmoral's eyes were as wide as saucers, and he laughed with excitement, touching the different objects, holding them in his hands.

"I think it's time we started planning," said Armon, and then he turned and jumped out the wide window. A moment later we heard whining, and Piggott was raised on giant hands over the windowsill. Scroggs followed, and then Armon climbed back into the clock tower and pushed all the armor aside so we might sit in the center of the room.

The eight of us sat in a circle — me, Armon, Balmoral, Yipes, Murphy, Odessa, Piggott, and Scroggs. Balmoral produced a map he'd been working on for many months and placed it in the center of the circle. It was drawn on parchment paper with black ink, and it detailed the position of each ogre.

"I can't read or write, but this drawing is about as close to perfect as I can get it. I would have shown it to you earlier, but with all the commotion, well —" Balmoral broke off, glanced at me, and looked down at the map. It took him a moment to get going again, but he had so much energy and passion that before long he was enthralled in the plan, taking us with him every step of the way. First he detailed all the events of the evening, giving special attention to the encounter with the ogre

163

and the way it had been destroyed. It was more than a little grotesque, the way Balmoral explained how easily the blade went into the top of the head, as if the skull were made of eggshell instead of bone.

"The first challenge will be hiding the fact that ogres are disappearing throughout the day and night. They check in with one another, not across sections so much, but within the forest or the Valley of Thorns or one of the other areas. They expect to encounter one another regularly. To overcome this problem we'll have to systematically take out each area, one at a time. The easiest areas to clear out will be the wharf and the forest. The housetops and the trees, combined with the weaponry Armon has provided, will give us an advantage.

"The guards that work for Grindall are all Castalians, and they are Castalians first. They have no weapons, but they do have two things we can use to our advantage: mobility and warning signals. I shall address the warning signals in a moment. As to mobility, some of the guards are actually assigned to patrol the forest along with the ogres. Others patrol the wharf, and still more include the City of Dogs in their rounds. To be fair, the rounds through the City of Dogs have been few and far between in recent years, as the dogs have become wilder and the dumping ground more uninhabitable. It's often forgotten for long stretches of time by both ogre and man. This will prove a good piece of luck for us."

Balmoral looked at Piggott and Scroggs uncomfortably, as if the dogs made him nervous or unsure, and then he addressed them directly.

"I can't understand you, but if you can understand me, know that your role in this conquest is of critical importance. Without you and your respective groups, we'll have no chance of winning the day."

Both Piggott and Scroggs sat tall and proud, and I was happy to see them as part of something so big, so important. Balmoral ran his hand along the map as he continued going through his plan.

"You see, here, at the gate to the City of Dogs, I can send a half dozen guards through in the morning. They will tell the ogre at the gate that it has been a while since the dumping grounds have been patrolled, and they plan to spend several hours checking it thoroughly. The ogres will let them go, thinking they are making a reasonable request, and I will send them directly to the clock tower, where they can arm themselves and take up positions in the trees here, near the edge of the forest." He pointed then to the area on the map where the forest met the City of Dogs.

"The rest of the armor should be taken to the active dumping ground and hidden. My people will smuggle the weaponry in the garbage carts as they come back in, leaving just enough debris in the carts to cover whatever they can hold. Dumping runs begin in the early morning every day and there is at least one delivery of debris every hour. By midmorning all the armor will find its way into the wharf. Once inside, a network of peasants will distribute the various items, and by the time the noonday sun is straight overhead, two hundred Castalians will be armed and ready for battle."

Balmoral's plan was beginning to sound like it would at least give us a fighting chance. I nibbled at some dried fruit as he went on, my head bobbing now and then from fatigue. I was very tired, but Balmoral remained so enthusiastic it was hard to imagine falling asleep.

"The forest must be taken first. It's the most critical early victory if we are to succeed. Now, as I promised, we have arrived back at the issue of the warning signals used by the guards. These are horns that can be blown at varying levels of sound. Blow hard, and the whole kingdom of ogres comes running. Blow soft, and only those ogres within a reasonable distance hear the warning. This tool can be used to our great advantage. The ten patrolling the forest are spread out, and we shall blow the horn very softly from the trees at the edge of the City of Dogs. One by one, or maybe two at a time, ogres will come to the rescue of the guard who calls the signal, and when they do, we shall attack them from above in the trees. The ogres carry the horns as well, and it is absolutely critical that we draw them in slowly, one at a time, so we don't encourage suspicion. These ogres have a great deal of arrogance, and they will blow a horn only if the situation is desperate.

"What we ought to be able to do is take out the ten in the forest first, then move to the edge of the forest here, where it meets the Valley of Thorns, and go about the same exercise once again, drawing the ogres along the Valley of Thorns into the forest where we will attack them. In this case, we are as far from the wharf and the Dark Tower as we can be while still finding ogres. These guard the outer perimeter, so we can blow the horn a bit louder, draw several at once, and take them down in groups of three or four."

"Yes, but how can we be sure, in either the City of Dogs or the forest, that the ogres will arrive directly under us so we can strike?" asked Yipes.

"A guard calls them in, and when the ogre or ogres arrive, the guard will guide them to where we are hidden in the trees above. It will simply be a matter of a well-placed diversion," Balmoral answered.

"The wild dogs," said Armon. "We can draw the ogres around a single tree with a pack of three or four wild dogs. All of their attention will be focused on killing the dogs, which will make our attack from directly above all the more surprising."

"Now you've gone and stolen my thunder. Bad giant," said Balmoral. This brought a smile to my face, the first I'd had in quite some time.

"It is unlikely that all of the ogres from the Valley of Thorns will be drawn into the forest," continued Balmoral. "I think we will count ourselves lucky if we get half of them, which would leave seven or eight more roaming around. The Valley of Thorns backs up against the forest trees, and often in the late morning the ogres take refuge from the heat by standing near the trees for shade. Unfortunately, we have no way of knowing which trees the ogres will stand near, so we must use the dogs once again.

"The wild dogs never roam outside the City of Dogs, and seeing a small pack of them attempting to pass into the Valley of Thorns will enrage the ogres. What remains of them will come to the edge of the trees — where we will be waiting. It will certainly be our biggest challenge; if we miss one of them we might just as well have missed them all. That one will blow his horn and the ogre barracks will blow open, unleashing an army we will never be able to overcome."

Everyone looked around the room at one another, sensing the enormity of the odds stacked against us. All I could think about was the ogre in that room with John and the others, how it had smelled and looked, the terrible sounds it had made. Only Balmoral and I had been so close to an ogre and seen its terrible rage. I was glad the others hadn't seen such things.

"This all must take place within a few hours tomorrow morning," Balmoral warned, "between dawn and nine o'clock. If the guards from the wharf are gone much longer, the ogre at the gate will become suspicious. There are other guards in the forest and in the Valley of Thorns who will help you. Once the forest is cleared, you'll have another six fighters. When you reach the last remaining ogres in the Valley of Thorns, you should have a dozen fighters in the trees. Along with Yipes and Alexa, that brings your total to fourteen."

"What about Armon?" I asked. "He's our greatest weapon. Where will he be during all of this?"

Balmoral pointed again to the map, this time to the cliffs beyond the City of Dogs, and looked at Armon.

"I'm afraid you must find a way to destroy the three ogres at the cliffs on your own. This will require straight hand-to-hand combat, three against one. And, worse, you must somehow make sure they cannot blow their horns." Balmoral glanced back at the map, then said, "I have had occasion to see this place. The cliffs rise high above the water, but how high no one knows. Even in the heat of summer the mist rises to hide the water below. The edges of the cliffs are solid underfoot and speckled with sharp rocks."

"I'll take Scroggs with me," Armon said. "Piggott and Odessa, you go with the others. Scroggs, bring six of your most trusted companions. Together we'll divert them one by one, draw them to the edge of the cliffs, and hurl them into the mist."

Armon was so certain, so sure, his voice like a slab of rock. It gave us a new measure of confidence we had previously lacked.

Balmoral nodded his approval of Armon's plan. "While the lot of you are at the business of clearing the forest, the Valley of Thorns, and the cliffs, I will guide my fighters on the wharf. The only way this works is if we strike at the wharf all at once, avoiding the gates to the Dark Tower in the process. The wharf is split into two sections, the forest end and the end nearest the Dark Tower. Five ogres patrol each — four on the castle side, since one was killed tonight. They are fairly regular about how they move around. An hour before dark, we will strike at the nine that remain and move the bodies off the street before darkness falls. I don't think the one we've killed will be missed in the morning. Often they wander into the barracks as a pack, and stragglers arrive later, occupied with some duty that keeps them out a bit longer. Before long, they fall asleep and think nothing of one another. However, by the time the next shift goes out, he will be missed, so we must strike immediately."

"Let's say for the moment that the plan works," I said. "The forty-four that remain in the barracks will wipe out all our effort as soon as they wake up. How will we deal with all of them at once?"

"As long as we stay away from the castle gate, the plan will work," answered Balmoral. "The sleeping ogres follow the same pattern every day. They wake, they eat, they march out to the gate, and then they disperse to the places where they must work and replace the ogres from the shift before them. In doing so, they follow the same road away from the gate and onto the wharf. Once through the gate there are twenty ogre steps, then a sharp turn and a long, narrow walkway with buildings on either side. It is here that we will attack them all at once, all but the ones who exchange places at the gate and around the Dark Tower itself. I have other plans for those fourteen. But the thirty-seven who walk the shadowy narrow road will have no idea what is about to happen to them. I'll have two fighters, each with swords, assigned to each ogre. They will be positioned along the tops of the buildings a few feet apart. A first strike all at once on every beast and a second just in case we miss our mark."

We all looked at Balmoral, his bulging eyes alive with victory, and we believed. We actually began to believe we could defeat the ogres, Grindall, even Abaddon himself. If we could do all that Balmoral suggested, there would only be the six ogres at the gate, the eight from around the castle, both the ones that had been on guard and the new four who had come to replace them. Those fourteen, plus the ten in the castle. With Balmoral's plan, we'd gone from ninety-eight ogres to twenty-four in only one day. Still, even twenty-four ogres was a formidable army given their size and strength.

"I know what you're thinking — we still have four-teen outside and ten inside to deal with," said Balmoral, as if he were reading my mind. "The ogres at the gate will have heard the commotion and they will come run-ning. These will be easy targets for my fighters. But what of the ogres that remain around the Dark Tower? It is at this point we must take the tower by force. Two hundred armed Castalians, a hundred or more wild dogs, a giant of our own, all against what remains — eight giants outside and ten within the Dark Tower."

Balmoral paused and looked around the room, which was faint with light from our dying candle.

"I believe at this point we will have created an even fight, a fair fight, a fight that could go either way."

That was a far cry from no fight at all, and we unanimously agreed to Balmoral's plan. At last our preparations were complete. Balmoral went home to gather his forces, and I was able to lie down on the cold floor of the clock tower. As I lay there, just shy of sleep, thoughts of what we might find in the Dark Tower began to fill my mind. I began to wonder what Catherine would say when she saw me, if she was even alive. And I wondered for the first time what Grindall would look like, how he would act, what he might say.

Murphy stayed with me and we whispered about John for many sad moments, and then we both fell fast asleep, exhausted from all that had transpired since our arrival in the City of Dogs.

# CHAPTER 21

# THE DARK TOWER

The morning air was cool and pleasant, especially so given our location high in a tree at the edge of the forest, the smells from the City of Dogs somewhere off in the distance. Yipes and I sat next to each other, hidden in the leaves of a monstrous oak tree, fifteen feet above the ground. Murphy was up much higher, thirty feet or more, scouting the area for ogres. I seized my new sword firmly in my right hand and held onto a branch with the other.

I looked over at Yipes, a few branches to my right, and saw that he was preparing his bow. Unlike the Castalians, he was very adept with an arrow. After some deliberation it had been decided that his best weapon would be the bow. I glanced at another large tree across the way and saw that two Castalian guards had taken up their positions and were waiting patiently. Beneath them were three wild dogs milling around the base of the great tree.

Squire circled above, scouting the entire kingdom. I wished again that I could be her, seeing all that she could see, knowing the very position of each and every ogre.

"I knew John a long time," Yipes said, startling me. The two wild dogs below our own tree and Odessa

173

broke their nervous pacing to look up at the sound of his voice.

"He had a hard life," Yipes continued, a little softer, "but he never complained, never once that I can remember. Though he had never met you, he spoke of you often."

"What did he say?" I asked.

"He worried about you. He knew it was his greatest duty to protect you. This was the most important job that Warvold had ever entrusted him with. Until this journey I never understood what John was talking about, but now it seems clear that he knew all along it might cost him his life to make sure you were safe. He died protecting you, protecting the last Jocasta, which is precisely what he expected might happen." Yipes smiled at me then, his wonderful little mustache covering up his lip, and I was suddenly afraid of losing him, too.

"Did he ever tell you why he was imprisoned?" asked Yipes.

"No. I asked him once on our journey but he wouldn't tell me."

Yipes repositioned himself on a limb and fidgeted with his bow.

"There was a group of women and children living in the forest," he quietly explained. "The story goes that John felt especially sorry for the children, so much so that he raided the kitchens and stores of Ainsworth in search of food and clothing for them. This went on for some time, and he was very successful in his pursuits on their behalf — until he was captured and put in with the rest of the convicts."

"Is that really true?" I questioned, maybe a little louder than I should have. Yipes only nodded and before I could question him further one of the dogs beneath us barked in our direction.

"Quiet!" Odessa growled from below. Then we could hear the faint sound of the horn being blown by the guard standing off to our left. My heart was racing, my palms sweating as we waited for what the warning sound would bring.

We were all very still, and then Murphy came scampering down and held firm to the tree trunk at my side.

"Hold tight, here they come," he said. This meant more than one, and I signaled two with my hand, to which Murphy nodded.

It was deathly silent, no wind in the trees, no sound of birds or other animals. The ogres were coming — I could sense them near. I began to hear the snapping of twigs and brush, and then I saw one of the hideous creatures come down the path, clearly irritated and looking around wildly for the guard who had called him. Another came bounding up behind him, scratching his head and grunting furiously. As they approached the guard, I looked over at Yipes. He had already drawn his bow and now held it firm, waiting for the moment when one or both of them stood beneath us.

As the guard and the ogres approached between the two trees, the dogs began barking uncontrollably, just as we had planned. The two ogres split, one taking the opposite tree, the other advancing on ours. He was monstrous, his head only a few feet below us as he approached. The dogs stayed right at the base of the tree, then moved back along its sides, drawing the ogre closer. The ogre drew his huge sword and appeared entertained by what he was seeing, excited about the prospect of putting his blade through these mangy animals.

I looked across the way again and saw that the ogre there had done the same and was directly under the tree jabbing and poking at the dogs with his sword. Down came a guard out of the thick of the tree, five feet over the head of the ogre. He plunged through the air, landing on the ogre's shoulders and thrusting the knife through the beast's head. At almost the same moment, Yipes fired his arrow at the ogre under our tree, but the ogre had glanced back, hearing the other ogre's scream over the incessant barking of the dogs. The arrow glanced off the ogre's head and down into his shoulder. He screamed an awful roar of pain and rage. We only had another moment before he would grab the horn and blow it, so Odessa's two companions went for the ogre's legs and chomped down hard and fast. The ogre kicked and flailed but the dogs were locked on and only death would get them off. The ogre reached down and grabbed both dogs at the neck. I yelled, causing the creature to look up as Yipes fired again, this time hitting the ogre directly in the forehead. To my astonishment, the arrow disappeared almost entirely into the ogre. He teetered a little to the left as if in slow motion, then fell backwards, crashing to the ground under the tree.

I came down from the tree quickly but kept my distance from the giant body, remembering what had happened to John. I was still surprised to see the ogre slowly sit up, then lean against the tree. He took his horn in his hand and tried to get it to his mouth. An arrow came from above and pierced the ogre's palm. I jumped in, grabbed the horn, and quickly moved away. The ogre wobbled once more and fell back to the ground, the dogs still holding hard at his legs.

I looked across the trail and saw that the guards had been victorious as well, and they were already calling us over to help drag the dead ogre into the thicket. It hadn't gone perfectly, but we had done it. We had defeated two ogres in the span of a few minutes.

The morning went along in much the same manner, the gruesome details of which I will not share in great detail. We were able to lure in all of the forest ogres. Besides the one wayward arrow Yipes had shot, we had other difficulties. Guards were lost, wild dogs were lost, and we arrived at the Valley of Thorns with six ogres still remaining. We had ten guards scattered through the trees and fifty or more dogs roaming beneath us on the ground, but the remaining ogres were not close enough to be taken. Before these ogres could think to blow their own horns, six of our guards made the warning sound, not loud enough for the wharf to hear, but louder than we had dared blow them in the forest. With so many horns going off all at once, the six ogres that remained didn't think to blow their own. Instead they ran to help, sure that every ogre from the forest would come running as well. When they arrived at the trees, the dogs began their barking and the arrows and swords began to rain down on the ogres. A few minutes later we'd taken what remained of the ogres in the Valley of Thorns.

All told, we lost thirteen dogs and two guards. Another guard was badly shaken when an ogre slammed him up against a tree, but he was able to continue on, a few broken ribs not enough to keep him from the important work ahead. It was midmorning and we had achieved something miraculous, setting the stage for what we hoped would be greater victories in the hours to come. We raced back to the clock tower and found Armon and Scroggs waiting for us. They, too, had been victorious at the cliffs by the sea. One was taken while he lay sleeping, the other two lured to the cliffs by the dogs and pushed from behind by Armon.

Balmoral had thought of everything, and when we arrived back at the clock tower, Margaret was waiting for us with fresh uniforms. The guards removed their bloody, stinking clothes and replaced them with new ones. Then those who had joined us earlier in the day ran off toward the gate, no doubt to receive more weaponry and instructions from Balmoral on the wharf.

"I must go quickly," said Margaret. "I will bring word to Balmoral of your success. Stay here until an hour before dark, and then wait at the edge of the wharf in the trees. Remain out of sight until a fire is lit by the lake, and then come as quickly as you can."

We bid her good-bye and offered Piggott and Odessa as escorts through the City of Dogs, which she accepted.

Then we waited as the minutes turned to hours in what seemed an excruciating slowness. We ate and talked of our accomplishment, of what we would do on the wharf. We spoke of the black swarm that remained loose on the wind, hunting for Armon, and our fear for him as we advanced on the castle. The thought of this perfect creature mauled by a thousand bats was unbearable, and I begged him to stay behind. But he was no more willing than I to remain in the City of Dogs while the decisive encounter took place at the Dark Tower.

In due time the hours turned the day to an orange dusk and the whole of our army made way for the edge of the wharf — dozens of wild dogs, a very small man, a squirrel, a girl, a smattering of Castalian guards from the forest and the Valley of Thorns, and one giant. We were not what you might hope to see coming around the corner to save the day, but together we had defeated twenty-eight ogres, and we walked with confidence, knowing we at least had a chance of winning the day. The dogs in particular had a new pride in their step and in the way they held their heads. I was happy for them, for the sense of purpose they enjoyed.

We waited as instructed, quietly looking for the flame against the lake as the day melted away on the horizon. In the distance I could see the Dark Tower, and I imagined Grindall himself standing atop the highest point, looking down on his wretched kingdom, thinking all was well as the sun tipped down and out of sight against the shimmering of the lake.

"There it is, the fire," said Yipes, who sat on Armon's shoulders. With that, we were moving fast, the whole lot of us, the dogs leaping out in front and running with all their might, Armon's huge strides keeping pace, Yipes and Murphy riding on his shoulders. This left me at the rear, running as hard as I could to keep up and falling behind quickly.

"Come on, Alexa! Run!" yelled Yipes. And so I did. With everything I had in me, I ran, sword drawn, onto the wharf and toward the Dark Tower.

I arrived at the narrow road to find ogres and Castalians strewn all about. It was a sea of bodies large and small. From the looks of it, the Castalians had triumphed. As I dodged and ran down the narrow road, I heard the dogs barking and growling. It was a ferocious noise that chilled my bones.

I came around the last corner and saw that the gate blocking the road to the Dark Tower had been breached.

All of the Castalians, dogs, and guards had gone through and were laying siege on the ogres at the base of the tower. All at once I was struck by the evil of this place — the dark spire against the night sky, the single flame from a window far above, and the silhouette of a man who looked down upon the war that raged at his feet.

I was terrified by this place. I had some trouble breathing, and I began to wobble back and forth where I stood. Then the strangest thing happened. I heard a voice, one unlike any I'd heard before, like the wind rolling in one ear and out the other.

*It is you who must go, you have I chosen. There is no other.*

I heard the words as clear as a bell. They were firm, and they were not a request — they were an order. I began to walk, slowly at first, and then I was running again, to the long line of stone steps that led to the great wooden door of the Dark Tower. While the fighting continued below, I kept running, bounding from step to step. I didn't look back, I only ran and ran until I stood on the last stair and gazed up to see a hulking beast of a door, big enough for an ogre to walk through upright, a layer of iron bars before it, and in front of that a wicked ogre with a spiked maul in his huge left hand.

"Out of the way, Alexa!" It was the booming voice of Armon, who had come up behind me unnoticed. He was standing on the steps, ripping a giant stone from its mortar where it protruded from the Dark Tower and formed

181

part of the entryway. The stone was so big, a square mass he could barely get his huge arms around. He pulled it free and raised it over his head, advancing on the door. Then he threw the stone with all his might into the ogre, knocking him back and smashing him through the bars. With tremendous effort Armon picked up the stunned ogre and hoisted him over his head. With a loud cry he threw the foe over the edge of the stairs.

I crawled up onto the stone banister to look over the edge and saw that the ground lay fifty feet below. Torches lit the night well enough to see that Balmoral, the dogs, and the Castalians were overtaking what remained of the ogres. Soon they would have control of the tower. I jumped down and stood at the door, the bars mangled but standing.

"Step aside, Alexa," Armon said, taking the huge stone and throwing it once more. This time the door itself blew apart at the center.

The entrance to the Dark Tower lay exposed. Inside, darkness and the flickering of torches against barren stone were all that could be seen.

# CHAPTER 22

# VICTOR·GRINDALL

I stepped carefully inside the doorway, then Armon ripped away what remained of the bars and the door and strode in behind me. It was damp and musty inside, weak flames from a few torches the only light I could see. Everything was dark stone and eerie shadows. I could still hear the dogs barking below, and there was a soft breeze blowing through the exposed opening behind us. Still, there was no mistaking the whispery voice that came on the wind once more.

*The black swarm is near. Send Armon away to the cliffs at the edge of the sea.*

The thought of Armon morphing into an awful ogre terrified me even more than staying within the Dark Tower alone. I looked up at Armon and beckoned him to lean down to where I stood.

"What is it, Alexa?" he asked, seeing my concerned expression.

"The black swarm is near, Armon," I said. "You must go to the cliffs and wait for us there."

He stared at me a moment and then took my shoulders in his enormous hands.

"It is said that the last stone would bring the word of Elyon himself. That the one who possessed it would hear

183

his very voice," the giant said reverently. "Have you heard this voice?"

I looked down and grabbed hold of the leather pouch that kept my Jocasta hidden.

"I believe I have," I whispered. "You *must* go right now, before they come for you. Run, Armon!"

Armon rose quickly, turned for the door, and lumbered away. As he disappeared into the darkness, I heard voices. At first distant, then closer. I drew my sword . . . only to lower it in relief when I saw two little heads peering around the edge of the broken door. One was furry and twitching, the other mustached. It was Murphy and Yipes, and they bounded into the open space of the tower. Armon dipped his head back into the doorway.

"It's up to the three of you now. You must save Catherine and put an end to Grindall once and for all," he said.

"Go! Go to the cliffs and do it quickly!" I yelled back. Armon nodded, turned away, and disappeared into the darkness, leaving Yipes, Murphy, and me alone in the gloom of the tower.

"A fine mess we've gotten ourselves into," said Yipes. "I suppose there's nothing left but to go as high as the stairs will take us . . . or down into the dungeon."

Murphy was already several paces ahead of us, sniffing at the stone floor and darting from side to side. There were two enormous sets of stairs, one going down and one up. The landing itself was circular, empty except for the two torches that hung along the walls. I immediately thought of going down until we reached the dungeon, rescuing Catherine, and running away. Then I remembered the solitary figure at the top of the spire, standing at the window, watching his kingdom crumble all around him. If we were to put an end to Grindall, we'd have to find him first.

"We're going up," I decided. "He's at the top, only a few flights away. The dungeon can wait." The stone steps outside had led us to the very center of the tower — fifty feet below and fifty feet above. Something told me we were meant to find Grindall waiting for us at the very top of the spire.

Murphy was on the sixth step before I could say another word, moving fast for the next level, staying close to the wall where the shadows lurked. Yipes and I followed quietly, winding around the inside of the tower, the sounds from below growing weaker as we went. After what seemed like a very long time, we came to a landing and yet another door. I thought it odd that the door was ajar, but Murphy thought nothing of it and scampered right through.

I pushed gently on the door and it opened slowly on squeaking hinges. When there was just enough room to put my head through and see inside, I smelled the ogres — that terrible smell of wet, rotting flesh. It was coming from behind us, and as I turned back to look, the door flew open and we were pushed inside. Yipes and I both fell to the floor, surprised. The door was slammed behind us, two of the biggest ogres I'd seen standing before it, placing a huge wooden beam across the middle and barring the door from anyone who might seek to enter.

"I don't see how this can get any worse," Yipes mumbled. But then we both looked into the dimly lit room and saw that eight more ogres, all of them bigger than any we'd seen before, stood in the room. Four of the beasts were against one wall, four against another. Between them stood a single stone chair where a man in a flowing dark purple cape sat, head down, his long black hair cascading over his face so that his features could not be seen.

"Guess you were wrong," I said.

The man in the chair looked up, crazed, his head tilted to the left. His skin was deathly pale, as if he hadn't seen the sun for years and years. His eyes bulged miserably from their sockets, full of rage and deceit, his gaze locked on the leather bag that held my Jocasta. His brow was set low over his eye sockets, and, to my astonishment, when he saw me looking at him he bared his twisted teeth as though he were a wolf or a serpent. His thick lower lip hung down and a twinkle of drool marked the corners of his mouth. I realized then that Grindall — for this had to be Grindall — was not at all in his right mind. He pulled his upper lip back from his teeth in a sinister grin and bolted up from the chair. It was then that the ogres began to speak in their own language, filling the room with the sloppy, guttural sounds of groans and low roars. Grindall spoke to them in their language, and I was amazed to hear the sickening sounds he made as he commanded these creatures in harsh tones. They became still and, though their noisy, wet breathing remained, they were mostly quiet.

"You have caused me a great deal of difficulty, Alexa Daley," Grindall intoned, his voice sultry and deep now, almost hypnotic in its slow cadence. "However, you have also delivered something to me for which I have searched an awfully long time. How convenient that the last Jocasta hangs around the neck of a pitiable little girl, a mere child. I find it amusing that this is the best Elyon could do."

"Are you Victor Grindall?" I asked. He looked at me with such malice I had to turn away, and then his voice slithered out once again.

"Indeed I am. The tenth Victor Grindall, to be exact." His voice was measured and slippery. "And these are my servants, the most powerful of the giants, sworn to serve and go to their death at my choosing. A smelly lot, but as you might imagine, very useful in situations such as these."

Then I heard a glorious sound, for Balmoral and his

187

men had arrived outside the door, and they began beating on it with all their might.

My confidence surged.

"You're trapped," I said. "You and these few remaining ogres. A very large army is about to break into this room."

"Is that so?" he replied. "How convenient for me, since I intend to bring the whole tower down on top of them. I have no doubt my servants will keep that door shut until you and I finish our business."

He spoke again in that hideous, throaty voice and ordered two more ogres to the door. There were four there now, and though the door bounced on its iron hinges when the men on the other side battered it, it seemed unlikely that they would break through soon enough to save us.

Grindall advanced to the window and looked out, then returned his attention to us and leaned against the sill. Behind him I could hear a terrible sound on the wind. It was the sound of leathery wings and the shrill voices of a thousand dark creatures. The black swarm was coming, searching for Armon.

"You do realize the one who created all this is long since gone," Grindall taunted. "He's not coming back, not *ever*. He fancies other creations now. Humankind has been quite a disappointment to him. I must say, I can certainly understand his position on the matter."

The bats arrived at the window and swirled in the night air behind Grindall, their shrieking almost unbearable. Grindall turned to them and spoke.

"The giant you seek is near, somewhere down below. Find him! Take him captive and bring him to me!"

Grindall turned back into the room with a new look — a sort of delighted rage.

"The only one in command around here is me and the forces I control," he said. "All the violence going on outside that door is utterly pointless. I have long since grown weary of these wretched Castalians. They're dirty, lazy, practically useless to me." He gazed once again at the pouch around my neck. "All that matters is the stone."

"If the tower goes down, you go with it." It was Yipes, his voice startling me. He was showing even more courage than I would have given him credit for in such an unnerving scene. The wild dogs outside were barking and the men were pounding to get in. The smell of the ogres was astonishingly strong in the small space, and Grindall was laughing. It was an awful laugh, sinister and crazed, half human and half something else.

"I believe you are the stupidest little man I've ever seen," Grindall spat, his laughing trailing off and his tone becoming serious once more. He strode over to where Yipes stood and backhanded him hard across the face. Yipes fell to the ground, motionless, his head bleeding from the temple. Grindall stood over him and heckled grotesquely.

"Oh, I say, you really *are* quite impressive. Maybe I should pick you up and toss you out the window. It would be a pleasure to watch you fly through the air and break into pieces. Or maybe my giants would enjoy eating you for dinner. What do you think, Alexa? Shall we toss him to the giants?"

The ogres grunted and moved closer, stirring up the rotten air in the room. Grindall was much stronger than I had anticipated, and he picked up Yipes by the vest and tossed him across the room. An ogre caught him and eyed him hungrily.

"Take out the Jocasta and give it to me, Alexa," Grindall demanded. "Give it to me now or we'll finish your friend." He was out of his mind, looking at the pouch as if it were the only thing in the world he cared about, his arm held back and waiting to signal the ogre to dash Yipes against the stone wall of the room.

*Take out the Jocasta and present it to Grindall.*

I couldn't believe my ears. It was the whispering voice on the wind. Had Elyon given up? Had I failed him?

"Have I made a mistake coming here? Did I do something wrong?" I asked.

"Who are you talking to? *Give me the Jocasta!*" Grindall screamed, his dark humor gone, nothing left now but desire for the stone around my neck.

190

*"Give it to me!"* he screamed again. A moment more and he would take it from me by force.

I looked at Yipes, so small and helpless. Then I gazed around the room. All stone; ogres at every turn; one large, open window that faced the lake; a flickering torch at its edge. After everything we'd been through, if Grindall did as he said, the tower would fall and destroy everyone, including Catherine. Elyon would be defeated, once and for all, and the dark reign of Abaddon would travel across the whole of our land, devouring it until nothing good remained.

I took the leather pouch into my hand, opened it, and pulled the glowing Jocasta out for everyone to see. I held it up high, its orange glow filling the room and dancing off the walls.

Victor Grindall looked at it, laughed nervously, and reached out his hand to take it away. And that's when I realized Balmoral was right: Elyon saw everything, even things Abaddon could not see in all his terrible desire for the stone. At the very moment Grindall was about to touch the stone, Squire screeched louder than I have ever heard her screech, and flew into the room, her massive wings flapping, her serious eyes focused entirely on the Jocasta.

Startled, Grindall turned for a moment and saw Squire come in through the window. I watched as Murphy dropped from the beams that ran across the ceiling. As Grindall looked back to the Jocasta, he felt

Murphy's teeth dig deep into his outstretched hand. Grindall screamed and grabbed Murphy, but Murphy would not let go. While they struggled, Squire arrived at the Jocasta, took it in one of her great claws, turned sharp against the back wall, and flapped for the window. As she arrived at the opening to the outside, an ogre slapped down with his sword. Feathers and sparks flew around the windowsill, but it was no use for Grindall. The ogre had only grazed Squire's tail, and the last Jocasta was gone from the room.

Murphy let go and scampered up one of the walls, then perched atop a beam near the ceiling. The sound of dogs barking and men clamoring to get in grew louder. The four ogres were struggling mightily now to keep the door closed.

"The army is about to break in," I said. "Have you any last words before we take the Dark Tower and destroy the last of your evil ogres?"

Grindall looked on me with loathing, trying to hide what must have been extreme pain from the bite Murphy had given him.

"Such a dreadful child," he said, and then his voice rose louder and louder. "You've only made things worse. Elyon is never coming back. What you've done has enraged me even more. I was content to sit here in Castalia and keep Abaddon under control. But look what you've done — you've released Abaddon to the rest of the world. This tower can no longer hold his rage."

Then he turned to his ogres and commanded them.

"Go! Make way for the true king!"

It was unthinkable, but five of the ten ogres — those not guarding the door or holding Yipes — ran to the window and jumped out. The door was about to come down and the remaining four ogres grunted and howled uncontrollably in their effort to keep Balmoral's army out of the room.

"You have unleashed Abaddon, and he will not rest until he rules everything," Grindall vowed. "I would suggest you leave this place now. The Dark Tower will soon crumble into pieces. You must live so you can return the last stone to me."

Then Grindall grunted at the ogre holding Yipes. The beast held Yipes under his arm, went to the window, and jumped out. I screamed for Yipes, but it was no use. He was gone.

Grindall bent down and put his awful face a few inches from my own. He reached out with his bloody hand and touched my cheek, saying, "There is a place I haven't had need of for a long time, especially with Ganesh watching it so closely for me all those years."

"Ganesh worked for you?" I asked, newly amazed at Grindall's reach.

"Well, of course he did, you silly child. What do you

think, that I'm not aware of all that goes on in your pathetic little kingdom beyond the Dark Hills?"

The way he said it made me wonder if there were others under his command within Bridewell. But who?

I shivered.

"I'll give you three days to meet me in Bridewell," Grindall went on. "You bring me my stone and I'll give you back your friend. Trust me, Alexa — Elyon is not coming back. This quest you're on is futile. You can save your friend *and* you can have a place of power with me. Just bring me the stone."

We looked at each other for a long moment, then Grindall rose to his feet and called to the remaining four ogres. He turned for the window, ran, and dove out into the night air like the rest. As soon as he was gone the last of the ogres bolted from the room and ran for the window, leaving the door behind as it splintered and broke open.

I crossed to the window and watched as they fell through the air, falling for such a long time, and then landing in a giant pool behind the Dark Tower. The pool was attached to the lake by a canal, and from beneath the tower I could see torchlight moving, as if on a boat. Grindall and the ten ogres had escaped, and they would cross the lake into the Dark Hills, bringing their evil plans who knew where.

Balmoral was in the room. He knelt down and put his arm around me.

"Are you all right, Alexa? Why did you come up here without us?"

"He's taken Yipes," I said, unable to think of anything else.

Balmoral and a few of his guards advanced to the window just as Squire was returning, which scared them all back for a moment. Squire flew around the room and dropped the Jocasta in my hand, then landed on a beam and screeched loudly.

"She's telling us to get out of here," I said. "Grindall has some way of bringing down the tower. We've got to get everyone out and find the dungeon before the whole thing tumbles down."

"What are you talking about?" Balmoral asked. "He's gone — I can see his boat from here. It's already moving out onto the lake." Then he paused a moment, and we all felt the tower shake and wobble back and forth.

"Oh, no," Balmoral said.

Everyone was running out of the room and down the stairs as quickly as they could. Balmoral was one of the last to go and Scroggs remained at his side.

"Come on, Alexa!" Balmoral urged.

I turned to Murphy and called him to my shoulder. I replaced the Jocasta in its pouch, then jumped onto the windowsill and looked back at Balmoral.

"We're going this way," I said. Murphy looked at me as though I'd lost my mind, and Balmoral yelled back at me to get off the sill. Then I heard Squire come up behind me and I watched as she flew free into the air. Murphy and I followed out the window, into the night. I closed my eyes, hoping the water below would cushion our fall enough to keep us alive. We flew and flew, down toward the ground, and then everything was cold and dark, my body stinging from the impact.

## CHAPTER 23

# THE DUNGEON

I burst out of the water, the sting from hitting the pool with such force still hanging over my body. I hadn't touched bottom even though my ears felt like they might burst from the depth. The pool was much larger than it looked from above, and clearly it was very deep. I saw Murphy paddling with all his might for the shore, and then I looked down the canal toward the lake and saw that Grindall was already well on his way, the ogres rowing on both sides, the group of them disappearing into the night.

I waded to the edge of the pool and crawled up onto dry land. The hour was late and already the dew had begun to gather on the slope. Early morning would soon come. I was behind the tower, which was guarded by two high walls that ran from the tower to the edge of the water. This was a secret place, a place prepared for just such a day, a day when Grindall might need to escape quickly without being stopped by anyone on foot.

The tower rumbled above and a section of stone broke free into the air, toppling down and banging along the side of the great structure as it went. It was bigger than a grown man and landed with a loud thud behind the wall. It shook the very ground we stood on.

"What could Grindall have done to set the tower to fall?" I asked.

Murphy was running his paws over his tail, wringing the water out of it.

"He must have used the might of the ten ogres at the base of the tower," said Murphy. "Maybe he had this whole thing set up so he could jump and then remove stones that were made ready for just such a night. If the right stones have been pulled out at the base, it's certainly possible he could bring down the whole thing. In any case, we haven't much time before it collapses entirely. We'd better get moving."

We stood and began walking along the edge of the pool toward the tower, where a large opening gaped before us. The sunken cave was completely black inside, the water like a sinister dark syrup hanging low in the space. This must have been where the boat was kept, and it was our only hope of getting into the dungeon before the tower crumbled all around us.

I heard voices and shouting on the other side of the wall and saw the flicker of torchlight against the tower. Then a huge hand grabbed hold of the top edge of the barrier, and what must have been one of the last of the ogres pulled himself up onto the wall and stood upright. He did not see us, he only stood and howled, arrows sticking out from his legs and one arm, blood pouring off him from all over. And then something miraculous happened. Armon, whom I'd sent to the cliffs, jumped onto the edge of the wall and stood toe to toe with the damaged beast. Armon was every bit the powerful fighter and he quickly overcame the ogre. The two fought with swords for a brief moment, and then Armon knocked the ogre back off the wall, away from us, and I could hear the Castalians below overtake him.

"Throw me a torch!" Armon yelled to the people below. A moment later he had the light in his hand. He then jumped down on our side of the wall, and in three quick strides stood towering over Murphy and me.

"Why aren't you hiding at the cliffs?" I asked. I was happy to see him but also worried.

"I stayed there for a while and watched the swarm making its way toward me, but before it reached me it turned," said Armon. "It appears it has fled to the lake, following Grindall and the ten remaining ogres."

Looking out over the water, it did seem as though a black cloud hovered over Grindall's boat, a cloud slightly darker than the rest of the night hanging over the lake.

Armon motioned behind him. "That ogre on the ledge there, he was the last of them remaining here. The Castalians are free at last."

Just then the tower wobbled once more, this time with more force, and another stone tumbled off the top section to the ground, larger this time and accompanied by a group of smaller sections that were torn loose as well. From over the lake I heard the distant laughter of

Victor Grindall, who was roaming free and heading toward my homeland.

"We have to reach the dungeon and save Catherine," I said. "We must hurry!"

Without another word Armon was moving, the torchlight dancing on the walls of the cavernous opening. He stepped into the water and was quickly in past his chest.

"Grab hold of my shoulders!" he yelled.

Murphy scampered up my body and sat on my head and I waded out into the water. I wrapped my hands around Armon's thick neck and he began to swim into the darkness, one hand holding up the torch, the other paddling us into the murky cavern. Before long Armon was walking again, and I dropped down off his shoulders and waded until I could stand. When I reached the place where Armon stood, there was a stout wooden door built into the stone base of the tower. It was marred with age and half decayed from the moisture, but it was still a terribly strong-looking barrier to our entrance.

Armon handed the torch to me and ran his fingers along the edges on the top and sides of the obstacle before us. The tower rumbled once more and dirt showered down on us. I closed my eyes, certain that we'd missed our chance, sure the tower was about to come down on us. But once again it held, not ready to fall to pieces just yet.

"Hold the torch down here," Armon said. I angled it down near his feet and illuminated the muddy earth at the base of the door. There was enough of a gap that Armon could get both of his hands underneath.

"Stand back," he said, crouching down and waiting for me to move away from the door. There was no place else to go, so I backed down into the water until I stood with only my head and arm protruding out. Murphy's paws had hold of clumps of my hair, and he tightened his grip with each step back into the water until I finally had to tell him to stop.

Armon used all his strength to lift the door up and out. He groaned loudly, the sound echoing through the cavern. The door broke free and Armon fell back into the water just in front of me, sending a massive wave of water over my head. Armon caught hold of my arm and dragged me back to the door, both of us dripping wet, the torch a black ball of smoldering ash. Murphy had lost his grip and paddled up behind me.

Through the opening there was a long stone hallway and torches along the walls. I picked up Murphy, whose wet fur felt like a soggy bit of green moss, and I ran through the entrance and down the hallway with its flickering light. Armon was close behind, and as the tower trembled above us we descended the stairs into the dungeon. Huge wooden beams lined the ceiling, creaking under the pressure of the tower. There were no longer any moments of silence — the tower was coming down, and it was coming down in a matter of minutes, if not seconds.

We rounded a corner on the stairs and then landed on a dirt floor in a long room. On either side were arched stone entryways, five on each side, and between each entryway were torches. At the end of the room, there was a large chair and a set of keys hanging low from one of the legs. Next to them was a narrow flight of stone stairs that led up into darkness. Armon took one of the torches and walked along the length of the room, flashing the light toward the entryways, discovering that each was covered with thick iron bars. These had to be the dungeon's cells.

"Catherine!" I screamed, but no one answered. We went a bit farther, past the first two sets of cells, which were empty. And then, at the third cell on the left, we found a body hunched over in the back corner. Armon handed the torch to me and took the thick bars in his hands. He groaned madly, trying with all his might to pull the bars away, but his strength was beginning to diminish with exhaustion. He stepped back with a puzzled look on his face, as though he couldn't imagine such a thing as bars he couldn't bend. He set his brow, grabbed the bars again, and tried once more to pull them apart. Just as the bars began to separate with agonizing slowness, Murphy spoke.

"Theeth wight helph." He held the ring of keys between his teeth, and Armon looked down at little Murphy and smiled.

"You make up for lack of size with impressive resourcefulness." Armon took the keys, inserted one of them into the lock, and swung open the iron gate.

I ran into the small, damp cell, calling Catherine's name over and over. I knelt down beside the frail body, all crumpled over and dirty. Armon bent down and entered the cell with me, his huge presence nearly filling the space on its own.

I touched the body, shook the shoulder, and pulled the rumpled hair back from the face. I knew immediately that it was her. It was the woman I had known as Renny Warvold, who my adventure had taught me was Catherine. She was skinny to the bones and barely breathing, but it was definitely Catherine. She opened her eyes then, and looked at me with such joy I could hardly keep from hugging her frail body. It broke my heart to see her in such agony.

"Alexa?" she whispered.

Armon moved me aside, picked up Catherine, and strode out of the cell. The walls were beginning to crumble and the whole room was filled with the noise of impending doom. I got the message loud and clear: There would be time to reacquaint ourselves later. To my astonishment, Armon turned back toward the cells we had yet to check.

"Armon, where are you going?" I yelled. "We have to get out of here or we'll never make it."

And then it happened. The most miraculous thing I could have imagined in my most fanciful dreams. Murphy had gone out ahead while we tended to Catherine, and he had delivered the keys to another cell, which was now open. As we approached the archway to that last cell on the left, a man slowly walked out into the torchlight. He had a long, white beard, he was thin but strong-looking, and I recognized him immediately.

"Right on time, dear Armon. Although you might have moved it along a pinch given that the tower is about to fall on our heads."

Armon bowed low with Catherine in his arms. "My apologies, Mr. Warvold."

It couldn't be. How could Warvold be alive? Ganesh had poisoned him. He was dead. I had been there — I *knew* he was dead. His notes had led us all the way to where we now stood. Could it be that he had been here waiting for us all along, somehow alive all this time?

"It can't be," I said.

"How is she?" said Warvold, ignoring my quiet plea, staring at Catherine. He touched her softly, probably for the first time in years.

"She'll be fine," said Armon, and he threw Warvold over his shoulder and ran out of the room as fast as he could. I ran behind and caught Warvold's eye in the dancing light, watched his white hair springing up and down over his face as he bounced through the room. He winked at me and smiled his beautiful smile, still the same. He even seemed younger than I'd remembered him. And in that moment I knew his voice like I hadn't known it before. I always knew he loved me, that there was something special about our relationship, but until I heard the words I didn't realize what I'd done.

"I knew you could do this, Alexa! You've turned the tide in our favor!"

As the walls came tumbling down, we ran from the dungeon, outrunning death, Catherine and Thomas Warvold with us once again. We emerged from the tower and swam through the pool, and then we kept on running along the wall toward the lake. When we were just to the edge of the lake, we stopped at the thundering sound of the tower falling, falling in a great heap on the earth. The sound was deafening, like waves crashing against the rocks in a storm. The time it took for the tower to fall seemed like forever, as if it were crawling to oblivion. It tipped to the left of us and then the bottom buckled out and the whole thing came tumbling straight down. As the dust began to clear we could see that the stairs leading up to the tower entrance remained, broken at the edge with a pile of rubble beneath them. And then the men and women of Castalia began to climb the stairs. In the dim light of morning we could see them, rising from the ground and walking up the stairs, waving hands and cheering as they went.

A new day was dawning for Castalia.

Armon set Warvold down and held Catherine out to him. She was awake now, the fresh air and the sound from the crash of the Dark Tower bringing her back to life. With my help she stood, and Warvold embraced her.

I looked across the lake and saw morning coming, and a dot on the horizon — Grindall and his ogres escaping into the Dark Hills.

# CHAPTER 24
# OVER THE CLIFFS

We stood in the clearing a moment longer, Warvold with his arm around me, Murphy jittering on his shoulder. Warvold had a troubled look in his eye and I could guess that our rest would be short-lived.

"We must move quickly. I'm afraid our work has only just begun."

Armon picked up Catherine again and we raced around the wall, hip deep in the lake. On the other side we found Balmoral, who Warvold also seemed to know.

"So nice to see you, Balmoral," Warvold said. "You look as though you've had a mighty good evening."

"That I have, sir, made all the better by the sight of you and Catherine."

"Balmoral, if I might ask a favor, could you bring the longest and strongest rope you can find to the cliffs right away? We'll meet you there and make our departure. Oh, and find John. He'll be coming along with us."

We all looked at Warvold hesitantly, unsure how to proceed. It was an awkward moment, and then Catherine spoke the words that nobody else would say.

"He's dead, isn't he? He died trying to save us."

Nobody could find the right response; we all just

looked at Catherine and Warvold and nodded our heads. But then Balmoral stepped forward.

"No, ma'am. That's not exactly right. He died trying to save more than the two of you alone. He died trying to save Castalia. And by the looks of that tower, he's done it."

Balmoral paused a moment, then continued. "I'm afraid Grindall has taken Mr. Yipes as well, and we don't know whether he's alive or dead."

"He's alive," I said. "Grindall told me he would keep him alive if I brought the last stone to Bridewell in three days."

Warvold was always composed and calm as a leader, but my statement alarmed him.

"We must move quickly," he said. "More than our little friend is in danger. If Grindall means to take Bridewell, the walls that remain around it won't be enough to hold him back."

"There's one thing more I should tell you," I said.

Warvold raised one eyebrow, listening carefully.

"Grindall said something about Ganesh working for him."

"That comes as no surprise," said Warvold.

"Yes, but after that, after he'd told about Ganesh, he said something that made me think there might be someone else working for him. Someone in or around Bridewell."

Warvold furrowed his brow and seemed to think this over while the soft wind blew his white hair back and forth.

"The thought had occurred to me," he said. "But I can't imagine who it might be. We'll have to be careful about who we trust in the days to come."

Warvold looked at Balmoral as if to say, *Shouldn't you be going?*

Balmoral stood a moment more and then all at once he seemed to remember what he was supposed to be doing.

"I'll be getting those ropes for you now," he said and then turned and ran away.

The rest of us walked quickly along the edge of the broken tower and spoke briefly to a few of the Castalians.

As we moved along Warvold kept looking at me, his bright green eyes blazing like I remembered from my childhood. He had such authority and grace. I felt no fear, only anticipation of what was to come in the days that followed.

Then I asked him a question that had been puzzling me.

"Warvold, why are we going to the cliffs? Won't we chase Grindall through the Dark Hills?"

"Too much work for a man of my age," he answered, though he seemed perfectly able by the way he kept up with Armon's pace.

Odessa, Scroggs, and Piggott came alongside us. Odessa had gained their respect and she was the biggest and strongest of the three by a healthy margin. Piggott and Scroggs seemed to have accepted her as the leader.

"It looks as though we've met with some success today," she offered.

"Not as much as we might have hoped for," I replied, and then I told the dogs about Grindall's escape and the unfortunate circumstances with Yipes.

When we arrived at the cliffs, the mist hovered as it always did a few feet below the rocky edge. We were not long in waiting for Balmoral, who arrived with two of his men carrying a long, thick rope between them.

I looked out over the edge. At every locality where ocean meets land there are the cliffs of black jagged rocks. If you look over the edge there lies a mist a few feet below, so thick you can't see the water. As far as the eye can see, nothing but white, puffy mist, as if we hang in the clouds and to step off the edge would leave us falling for days. If not for the violent sound of the waves against the rocks somewhere far below, one might suppose our lands were an island in the sky.

"There you are, then. Enough rope to tie up a herd of sheep," said Balmoral, interrupting my thoughts.

"Tie it to that rock, and make sure the knot is as tight as can be," Warvold ordered. He was pointing to an enormous stone jutting out of the ground about twenty feet back from the edge of the cliff.

Balmoral and his guards, with the help of Armon, did as they were told. A few minutes later they walked over to the rest of us, a few feet from the edge of the cliff and the mist below.

"Now throw the rope over the edge," Warvold continued. Balmoral looked at him as if he'd gone mad, not sure what to do.

"Throw it! We've got no time to lose," Warvold insisted.

Balmoral threw the rope over the edge. It was very long, maybe a hundred feet, and it fell into the mist to places unknown, places none of us had ever seen.

"What's everyone standing around for? Down we go! Roland is waiting!" said Warvold. "Armon, you go first with Odessa under one arm and Catherine on your back. We must get you out of sight before the bats return."

The largest and wildest river in The Land of Elyon was the River Roland, so named for the only person who had ever tried to sail it. Roland spent twenty years building a boat he called the *Warwick Beacon*, then disappeared down the pounding waves of the river into the Lonely Sea before I was even born. Nobody had seen or heard from him since. Everyone assumed he'd failed in the attempt and died long ago, the *Warwick Beacon* smashed into pieces against the rocks.

"Roland?" I asked. "Roland and the *Warwick Beacon*? Is he really down there waiting for us?"

"Well, he'd better be," answered Warvold. "I told

him to be there waiting on just this kind of day. If he's not there, I'll be awfully disappointed."

And then, quick as you please, he walked over to the rope, grabbed hold of it, and was gone over the edge with a smile, not another word spoken.

Catherine held up her arms to Armon as soon as Warvold was out of sight. Armon picked her up and placed her on his massive shoulder. He looked down at the two dogs and Odessa.

"Odessa, this could be a little uncomfortable. I apologize." The giant reached down with one arm and grabbed Odessa around the middle, pulling the wolf in close to his side. Then Armon took the two of them to the edge of the cliff, grabbed the rope with his one free hand, and disappeared into the mist, leaving the rest of us standing dumbstruck.

"I don't know about this," said Balmoral, shaking his head. "How can we be sure Roland is down there?"

Murphy shrugged, twitched his tail back and forth several times, and scampered down the rope. Piggott and Scroggs peered over the cliff, the jagged rocks jutting in wild directions, and watched as Murphy slid out of sight.

I looked at Balmoral and he looked at me. We stood on the lonesome cliff with the two dogs and contemplated what to do. I could see in Balmoral's eyes that it wouldn't be long before I was standing at the edge of the cliff alone. He looked back at the lake and the wharf, and I can only imagine the flood of emotions that over-took him.

"These years with Grindall ruling over Castalia have been hard going indeed," he said. "We have to stop him. We're the only ones who know how dangerous things have become. Nobody else will believe us."

He shuffled his feet back and forth in the grass.

"Warvold said it would only take a few days. I'll probably be back in a week." He looked at the two men who had stepped back and were waiting a stone's throw away and yelled to them.

"Tell Mary and Julia I had to go save the world with Thomas Warvold. I'll be back in a week's time." The two men ran off in the direction of the wharf. Balmoral turned and grabbed hold of the rope. He slithered down along the cliff's edge and vanished into the white puffy mist like the others.

I stood on the cliff alone with Piggott and Scroggs. It was oddly quiet as I looked back toward the lake, the sun up and the heat coming on quickly.

"I think this is what they call a leap of faith," said Piggott, and then he motioned to Scroggs and the two of them wandered off in the direction of the City of Dogs. I wondered what would become of them in this new Castalia, what would happen to the rest of the dogs. They'd fought with courage, but how long would the Castalians remember what these sick creatures had done for them? It seemed more likely that the City of Dogs would remain their home.

*A leap of faith.* All at once I was terribly tired. When would my duty be through? Could I ever hope to sit by a fire and talk with Catherine and Yipes and Warvold? The Land of Elyon was a much bigger and scarier place than I'd thought it would be.

*The Lonely Sea is the only way to the Tenth City.*

The voice on the wind was the only assurance I needed. I held my Jocasta in the safety of its leather pouch and looked one last time at the fallen Dark Tower. The people were celebrating, free from Grindall and the ogres. It was time to go.

I crawled down, took hold of the rope, and lowered myself slowly into the white fluffy haze.

# CHAPTER 25

# THE CHASE BEGINS

It was wet and slippery against the cliff, so my feet kept sliding off, knees and elbows banging against the hard surface. The mist was also wet, covering my hair and face with a soft layer of moisture that felt cool and made my lips taste salty. The mist was so thick I could hardly see the rope in my hands as I descended farther, more aware by the moment that I would never have the strength to turn and go back.

I heard voices from below, muffled by the quiet but constant slapping of water against rocks, the foamy sound of liquid seeping back into the earth. As I continued my slow descent the mist began to clear, and then all at once it was gone entirely. I looked up and saw a thick white layer that seemed to go on forever out into the open sea, a ceiling of misty wet clouds hovering fifty feet off the water. Then I looked down, and to my astonishment there was a vessel, a rather large one, bobbing on the surface of the water. It was impossibly close to the edge of the cliff, so close that it seemed to me it must have crashed against the rocks, water flowing into its belly.

As I approached the deck of the boat I realized that the cliff fell away into an open cave, the boat sitting halfway inside, perfectly safe on the waters of the sea.

Armon bid me to jump with fifteen feet remaining, and how could I resist the chance to jump into a giant's arms?

A man appeared from the front of the boat, a man I'd never seen but knew without hesitation. It was Roland. He looked salty from the sea: tattered clothes, long yellow hair and beard, leathery skin, and piercing cobalt eyes. He wore an odd leather hat on his head, and the sleeves of his shirt were neither short nor long but somewhere in between. His feet and ankles were bare and looked as though they had lacked cover for a very long time, the white curly hairs of his lower legs fidgeting in the wind as he came. He held a platter in his hands with dried fish and bread. He stood among us, and I got the feeling that he was the only crew member left.

"Sorry to hold things up, Thomas," he said. "I had to check the anchors, make sure we weren't going to swerve into the cliffs. She's a good vessel, but the *Warwick Beacon* needs a bit of babying to keep her afloat."

"I completely understand," said Thomas, looking more energetic by the moment.

"Roland has kindly prepared some food for us, and none of us are more excited to get to it than Catherine and me. Shall we eat, then?"

Roland set down the tray in the middle of us. Armon was the first to grab for it. He took bread and fish and presented the food to Thomas and Catherine. I found out later that Roland had been at sea for thirteen years, periodically drifting right near the place we were. For the past

216

year he'd been waiting around the very cliffs that rose above us. In the cave he'd found a fresh spring for water, and he'd always had plenty of fish to eat. The bread was a treat, the flour and oil taken from holdings he'd stored in the boat before departing. There is much to tell of the making of the vessel, the long years at sea, and the adventures Roland enjoyed. But those tales are for another time.

Warvold began to speak and told a great many things, the most important of which I will share with you now.

First he told us something that should come as no surprise: Roland and Warvold were brothers — one the great adventurer by land, the other by sea. There were many secrets between these two. They had managed to send messages to each other by choosing places where Warvold would drop a rope with a bright red flag, meager supplies, and word of what was happening above. Roland also sent messages to his brother, but Warvold mentioned little of these, preferring to keep them a secret.

The very last message Roland had received had come at the bottom of the cliffs at Lathbury, my own hometown. The message instructed Roland to be waiting a year later beneath the cliffs at the farthest western tip of The Land of Elyon, where another red flag would be hanging near the water's edge. The hanging of the flag was a task Armon was sent to accomplish when Warvold left on his journey to rescue Catherine. At the same time Warvold left the letter for me with Yipes, telling him to wait a year before giving it to me. It was Warvold's hope that he could subdue Grindall on his own without help. As it turned out, Warvold was captured and sent to the dungeon, where we eventually found him.

I was, of course, curious as to why he'd been so bold as to attempt this mission on his own without help. To that he replied matter-of-factly, "What are you talking about? I planned for all sorts of help, as you can see by looking around you. Roland, Armon, Murphy, Yipes, Balmoral — and you, Alexa. I hoped I wouldn't need anything more than my own ingenuity, but Grindall proved more clever than I had expected. Still, I was realistic about my chances. I thought I might need help from each of you, but I only wanted to have it when I was absolutely sure I would need it." Once again I was struck by the brilliance of this man. Only he could have planned how each of us would become involved, keeping us out of harm's way until he knew he'd failed in his attempt to save Renny.

Then Warvold told us how he'd managed to fake his own death on the night when he'd walked out to the wall with me. He was aware of Ganesh and his plot to overthrow the walled cities, but Warvold had larger problems to deal with. Catherine had been taken, and he was determined to go to her, to reveal all he knew to the right people at the right time, to free his wife and the Castalians from the hand of Grindall.

And so he'd created an elaborate plan that started when Ganesh attempted to poison him. Warvold recognized the danger and instead took a potion, a potion of his own making that slowed his breathing and his heart to almost a stop. Only Grayson was in on the plot, the trusted librarian and dear old friend. In the days after Warvold's so-called death, Grayson was the one who took care of the body and placed it in the burial box. While everyone else was mourning, the two of them ate toast and strawberry jam and sipped tea in the secret places of the library. When the time came for the funeral, Warvold took the potion again and slept through it all. And finally, when Grayson prepared the body for burial, he replaced Warvold with a long bag of dirt, and sent Warvold on his way.

"I have only a little more to tell you, and then we can put up the sails," Warvold said, that hopeful look on his face, the one that could put human and beast to work on whatever he wished them to do.

"We have struck a great blow to Abaddon on this day, but there is much left to complete. Grindall runs free and we are the only ones who can stop him. He carries with him one of our dearest friends. We are the only ones who can rescue Yipes.

"In the coming days, we will sail the sea beneath the mist and make our plans. We must be as crafty as foxes, for Grindall and the ogres live only to destroy us. The only thing Grindall cares about is the stone and the devastation he can leave as he goes looking for it."

Warvold stopped a moment and measured his next words carefully.

"Nicolas, Grayson, and Pervis — if they read the letter you left for your father, they'll be expecting Grindall and the ogres. And your father, too, Alexa. There is much you still don't know, and I had my reasons for keeping things secret. The fate of The Land of Elyon hangs around your neck, and this burden must be carried with the help of your friends if we are to succeed."

Warvold picked up a loaf of bread and tore a piece out of it, then he said the last of what he needed to say, which was something I already knew.

"With the help of the last stone, we must find the Tenth City."

I felt then that none of us, not even Warvold, knew why we had to go there. Some duty awaited us beyond the Sly Field in this secret place, but we could only guess at what it was.

When Warvold was finished, Roland raised the anchor and Armon got into the water and swam, pushing us away from the cliffs and into the soft wind. The sails went up next, and we were on our way to new adventures, ones I didn't have the strength to even consider until a new day. As the breeze carried us on blue waters I'd only imagined in my past, I curled up on the deck with an old blanket beneath my head. It was cooler under the mist, still warm, but nice. Murphy curled up in a ball at my side and I gently ran my hand across his body.

I whispered words into the wind.

"Don't give up, Yipes. We're coming for you."

And then I was asleep and rocking on the waves, riding the water toward home, enjoying the quiet company of the Lonely Sea.

It would be the last quiet I would know for some time.

*To be continued . . .*

# COMING SOON

## The Land of Elyon Book 3

### *The Tenth City*

Alexa Daley is lost at sea — drifting perilously close to the cliffs — and a storm is coming that threatens to tear the *Warwick Beacon* to pieces.

Armon, the last of the giants, is tracked relentlessly by the black swarm, whose aim is to turn him against Alexa and thwart her pursuit of the Tenth City.

Yipes is held captive by an evil band of ogres, his fate unknown.

And The Land of Elyon has begun to fail, poisoned by the evil that creeps across the Dark Hills and into Bridewell.

As she moves toward a thrilling conclusion, Alexa must find a way to overcome the Lonely Sea, rescue Yipes from the clutches of Victor Grindall, and unlock the mystery of the Tenth City. But can she find the answers she needs in time to save The Land of Elyon?

# ABOUT THE AUTHOR

PATRICK CARMAN maintains that he does not now have, nor has he ever possessed, a Jocasta or any other type of gemstone that offers the power of interspecies communication, telepathic or otherwise. Parties interested in obtaining such a stone are well advised to look elsewhere.

Mr. Carman does, however, speak to young people of his own species, sometimes aloud and sometimes in print. He makes his home in the wilderness of eastern Washington and insists that it is a rather ordinary home and is not, in fact, surrounded by stone walls.

Mr. Carman plays no musical instruments, but he has been known to torture dinner guests with attempts on the harmonica. He divides his time between writing, public speaking, spending time with his wife and two daughters, reading, fly-fishing, paragliding, and snowboarding.

To learn more about
Patrick Carman and The Land of Elyon
visit:

www.scholastic.com/landofelyon